The NightWriter Review

Volume 1, Issue 1

Winter 2024/2025

SLONightWriters.org

SLO NightWriters
P.O. Box 3154
San Luis Obispo, CA 93403

Publishing consulting services generously provided by
SLO NightWriter Brian Schwartz.

At SelfPublish.org, we transform the self-publishing journey
for authors seeking specialized expertise to navigate the
complex publishing landscape. We offer a high-touch,
results-driven consulting service that simplifies the path from
manuscript to market.

Powered by AuthorDock, our innovative web-based project
management platform, and backed by over 15 years of
industry experience, we provide comprehensive support that
combines cutting-edge tools, personalized coaching, and a
genuine commitment to your best interests. Want to learn
more? Book a free 15-minute discovery call.

Brian Schwartz
brian@selfpublish.org
(805) 323-6706

San Luis Obispo, California

THE NIGHTWRITER REVIEW

Editor-in-Chief .... Harvey Ardman

Managing Editor .... Leanne Phillips

Fiction Editor .... Brenna Humphreys

Nonfiction Editor .... Carolyn Rohrbach

Poetry Editor .... Michelle Turner

Copy Editor .... Leanne Phillips

Publishers .... SLO NightWriters
Brian Schwartz

THE NIGHTWRITER REVIEW

Issue No. 1

Winter 2024/2025

Poetry

EDITOR'S NOTE

Welcome! Welcome! Welcome!

Hola, readers and writers,

Welcome to the very first issue of *The NightWriter Review*, the literary journal of SLO NightWriters, the writers' organization in San Luis Obispo, on California's Central Coast.

SLO NightWriters was founded in 1989. We currently have more than 130 members. Our organization includes everyone from ambitious amateurs, eager to get their works in print, to seasoned veterans, some having written dozens of published books.

Our members fall into three broad categories: writers of fiction (novels and short stories), writers of nonfiction (writers of memoirs and a wide variety of other nonfiction), and poets.

We offer monthly programs, featuring presentations by authors, agents, and editors. We also conduct biweekly critique sessions, during which writers can get their work critiqued by their peers and by more advanced writers and get the opportunity to review the work of their colleagues. The aim of these critique sessions: to help us support each other and to develop our craft.

Every year, we sponsor the Golden Quill Writing Contest, which awards cash prizes to the winning authors in each of our categories. It is open to both NightWriter members and nonmembers. For many years, we have published the winning entries online.

Now, for the first time in our history, we will memorialize the best contest entries in print in our new publication *The NightWriter Review*. It will also include entries of great merit that didn't win awards, as well as selections from our general submissions. We plan to publish annually.

Our intention: to provide readers with the finest, most memorable, most touching, most thoughtful, most entertaining, funniest, most provocative examples of the writing craft, work that our members have created, as well as work submitted to us by nonmembers, work that has never been seen in print before.

We hope that you find these pieces entertaining, instructive, and encouraging. We'd love to have you enter the Golden Quill Writing Contest and give us the opportunity to publish your best work. The 2025 contest will open April 1st. Our goal as a publication and as an organization is to inspire writers at all levels and to serve as a supporting connection between writers everywhere.

Good reading—and comments are welcome.

Harvey Ardman
Editor-in-Chief
The NightWriter Review

SOUNDS LIKE JONI MITCHELL

Fiction by S. S. Presby

"Sounds Like Joni Mitchell" was the first-place winner in fiction in the 2024 Golden Quill Writing Contest.

Buddy is dying today. It's a bad day for it, but it's happening. Sheldon didn't know what was going to happen afterwards, when there was no one. But he had to kill Buddy, because he loved the big guy.

Buddy lay in his favorite spot with his back against the wall, on a sheet of vinyl flooring that Sheldon had bought at Do-It Center and spread over the carpet to protect it from explosions. Buddy's legs trembled every few seconds, like he was running down his last deer.

"It's okay Sonny," Sheldon said softly. "It's okay, big guy."

Sonny was Buddy and Buddy was Sonny. His official vet name was Sonny. But over the years he had acquired a lot of names: Buddy, Big Guy, Beast, Bud Boy, Budoou, Buzzard, Buster, Buzzy, Buzz. But Buddy was the name they had used the most. He responded to all of them, to the feeling that lay underneath the names, to the love. They had given him a lot of love.

Sheldon sat on the floor with his back against the wall and his legs out in front of him. He rubbed Buddy's neck and cheeks softly.

"Sweet Buddy, sweet boy." Sheldon's eyes got hot. "My big guy!"

Buddy thumped his tail.

Thump-thump. Thump-thump.

Sheldon felt a rush of hot liquid fill up his belly. He leaned down and kissed the big dog's face. Buddy's breath was beyond rancid.

"Oh Buzz, you need a mint like nobody's business."

Thump-thump. Thump-thump.

Sheldon looked at his phone and the text from the euthanasia lady. She was on her way ten minutes ago.

"How about some turkey, big guy?"

Thump-thump. Thump.

Buddy's tail was getting tired.

Sheldon's mouth twisted down into a thin rail. "Take it easy, Buzz. I'll be right back."

The death lady had told him that it was fine to feed Buddy while she did the injections, so Sheldon bought two pounds of organic turkey from Sprouts. He walked stiffly to the kitchen, sadness making his legs seem far away. He jerked opened the fridge, and one of Laura's face serums fell over. Sheldon stared at the stoppered bottle lying on its side. Its screw top was tight, so none had spilled. Laura was always very neat. He picked up the bottle gently. Touching Laura's things hurt, made him crazy and pissed all over again.

He dropped the vial into the trash without reading the label.

"Guess you didn't really need that one." He said to the empty kitchen.

Sheldon took out the sliced turkey, set it on the counter, got out a plate and unfolded two slices. Then he snorted. "Fuck am I doing?" He dumped the whole lump of sliced turkey onto the plate in a two-pound pile and carried it into the front room. He tore off a hunk of meat as he walked and ate it.

He sat down on the floor next to Buddy with the plate in his lap. "That's some pretty good shit, my bud."

Thump-thump. Thump-thump.

Buddy's nose was still alive, still running fast and hopeful.

Sheldon broke off a small hunk of meat without bothering to unfurl a slice and held it front of Buddy's face. "Here you go, boy."

Buddy snapped forward too hard and faster than Sheldon thought possible.

Sheldon jerked his hand before Buddy's loving teeth snapped to the bone. He stroked Buddy's neck gently. "Okay Bud, it's okay, easy does it."

Buddy was blind from the cancer and his movements were stiff and erratic. Before he got sick, Buddy had weighed over a hundred pounds. Now his ribs poked out like sticks, but his coat was still thick. All the carnage was happening on the inside.

Sheldon rubbed Buddy's head and stroked his body until he relaxed. "That's a good boy, Bud, take is slow." Sheldon moved the turkey back into range, and this time the big dog took the bite gently.

"That's a good boy, just a little at a time, sweet guy."

Time slowed down. It was just Sheldon and Bud. He fed Bud small chunks of turkey and let time roll backwards. Let what used to be fill up his eyes.

He and Laura had gotten Buddy as a puppy from the Humane Society in Pasadena. They sat in the car after their initial intake interview, and Sheldon laughed his ass off while Laura imitated the humorless, nasally adoption consultant.

What kind of pets have you owned?

Do you plan to have children?

Why or why not?

How big is the yard?

What sort of surface?

How high is the fence?

What did your parents fight about?

Did they yell at each other?

Did they yell at you?

Was corporal punishment used in your childhood home?

Who is the Alpha in your pack?

Why?

Have either of you ever sought, obtained, or been subject to a restraining order?

How much physical interaction do you plan to have with the dog?

How about with each other?

What is the plan when and if you split up?

Do you drink or do drugs?

Why or why not?

Sheldon had laughed until his sides hurt. Until snot came out of his nose and he peed himself a little.

Laura said, "We could have a pet human a lot easier." She did a Groucho take with her eyebrows and Sheldon cracked up again. "Just take out the diaphragm and get busy," she said.

Sheldon held out another hunk of turkey, but Buddy was done. He laid his head down and was panting hard. His legs trembled like he was shivering.

"It's okay Buddy," Sheldon rubbed the dog's face and ears gently. "You're okay, sweet guy."

The rain had blown out about midnight, and a fist of arctic cold punched in behind it. Sheldon had set up a space heater next to Buddy's bed, and the air around them was warm, but Buddy wasn't panting because he was hot, he was panting because he hurt.

Sheldon set the plate of turkey on the coffee table. He pulled a Mexican blanket off the couch, laid it over Buddy, and sat back down.

"Pet human," he said out loud.

But there was no pet human for him and Laura. Never going to be.

A few months after they got Buddy, they had taken out the diaphragm and went all in on the pet human enterprise. After trying for more than a year, Laura had gone to the doctor and found out that her fallopian tubes were in tatters. She had undergone a painful medical procedure in an effort to open up the tubes. The doctors had essentially pumped fluid inside her and tried to blast open her lady bits.

Sheldon stroked Buddy's body gently under the blanket. He was so skinny. He puked up almost everything now. All that was getting fed was the fucking cancer. Sheldon kept touching the dog's hair, and memories blocked his eyes like dense evergreens.

He remembered the bathroom door.

It was a few months after the tube blasting, and Laura had missed her period. It was a Saturday. He heard the toilet lid close and, sixty seconds later, sobbing. A few moments later she came out of the bathroom crying hard.

"Oh babe, I'm sorry, so sorry," Sheldon said and tried to put his arms around her. But she pushed him away and thrust the home test in front of his face.

"Blue, but blue is positive," he said.

Laura was crying so hard she couldn't speak, but she let him hug her, and Sheldon felt his heart running out to the horizon in every direction all at once.

But that's how God has a fucking jolly. He, she, them, it—whatever— is fucking pitiless.

The embryo had lodged in Laura's left fallopian tube instead of the uterus. She was pregnant, and they were both ecstatic for about three weeks, until the pain got really bad and she started bleeding.

"What a fucking laugh," Sheldon said out loud, and Buddy's ears twitched.

Sheldon took his hand out from under the blanket and rubbed his own face and head, giving himself a little petting. He tried to breath, tried to let go.

Buddy had a deep tremor and his whole body shook.

"Oh Bud," Sheldon said and put his hand on the big dog's neck. The sharp smell of wrecked tuna and shit leaked out from under the blanket.

Sheldon's sigh was almost a laugh. "Guess that about sums it up."

The tech that did Laura's ultrasound was matter of fact. He nodded his head in confirmation. "Ectopic," was all he said.

Just that one word, "ectopic," like that should have explained everything, balanced off all their wild hope, dissolved away catastrophe.

They heard the heartbeat on the monitor. It was so strong, so clear. Swoosh-swoosh, swoosh-swoosh. Swoosh-swoosh, swoosh-swoosh.

Thump-thump. Thump-thump.

Buddy was thumping his tail in shit.

"Fuck," Sheldon said.

He got up and trudged to the service porch then brought back two buckets filled with warm soapy water, paper towels, and rags. He kneeled down and went to work with paper towels cleaning up the chunks and slicks of slime. Once he had scraped and dry-wiped as best he could, he used a rag and warm water to bathe Buddy's bum and then sopped up the shitty water with more paper towels.

Buddy's body stopped shaking, but his legs were still in full tremor.

"That's a good boy, Buddy. Such a good boy, it's over now. It's going to be . . .." Sheldon's voice caught. He took the mess to the kitchen, stuffed the shitty towels into the trash, put the buckets outside, pulled out the trash bag, and took it to the bin.

"Isn't there any way to move it," Laura had asked the tech. "It's only a few inches, a few centimeters." Her voice broke, and she pushed Sheldon away when he tried to hold her.

The tech looked at her like she was crazy. "It's ectopic," he said again, enunciating each syllable like they were morons.

Sheldon wanted to bash the tech's head with the ultrasound wand, do a violent non-consensual proctologic exam on the bastard.

"Like a transplant," Laura said. Her voice was animated by magical hope.

The tech shook his head and finished cleaning the instrument. Sheldon almost grabbed the guy as he left. He wanted to shake him and scream at him, make someone give them an answer. But it wasn't the tech's fault. It was nobody's fault really.

In bed that night Laura had said, "I want to name him."

Neither the doctors nor the tech had told them it was a boy, but Laura said she knew.

"He should at least have a name before he dies."

She was teetering, right on the edge of another crying jag. Laura sat up in bed, and her legs were trembling. She kept clenching her hands into fists and then unclenching them and laying them flat on top of the covers.

"What name do you want to give him?" Sheldon asked.

"Henry," she said. "After your dad."

Sheldon's dad had died a few months before, and even though his dad had been sick for a long time, Sheldon was having a hard time coming to grips.

"Sure," Sheldon said. "He'd like that."

"What about you?"

"I like it too."

Laura cried then, they both did, and they held each other for a long time. Until Laura had to get up and go to the bathroom.

Sheldon was standing over the trash bin, and the lid was open. He didn't know how long he had been standing there. He dropped in the bag of shit rags, closed the lid, and went back inside. He put in a new garbage bag and washed his hands.

He looked at his phone to check the time. The angel of death was getting close. Laura wasn't. Laura wasn't going to come.

Sheldon had messed up royally last night. He had gotten stoned enough to crack open his hurt and drunk enough to be stupid.

He had called her.

Lenny answered.

Lenny was younger than Laura. Lenny was taller than Sheldon. Laura met Lenny in acting class. Laura had known Lenny for about three years. Lenny had long hair. Lenny had pale blue eyes, and she had probably been fucking Lenny even when she and Sheldon were married because she had been working on a scene with him, and when she and Sheldon split up, Laura moved right into Lenny's apartment.

"Hello," Lenny said.

Even though it was Lenny's apartment, and he was calling Lenny's apartment, it threw Sheldon to hear Lenny answer the phone at Lenny's apartment.

"Hello," Lenny said again, louder and slightly irritated. "Look man, were not interested in any—"

"Hey. Sorry. This is Sheldon."

There was a pause, and Sheldon could hear Lenny breathing.

"Is uh, is Laura there?"

More breathing. Lenny used up a lot of air. "Just a minute," Lenny said.

The sound was muffled. Lenny probably had his big hairy hand over the phone. Lenny had a lot of hair, even on the backs of his big hands.

After a minute, Laura came on. "Hello." Her voice sounded far away, like she wasn't really listening, or was really tired, tired of all their sad history, or maybe she was stoned, or maybe she and Lenny had just fucked and she was feeling easy and relaxed.

"It's Sheldon."

"Yeah."

"Uh, I just wanted to tell you that Buddy, uh, Sonny is. I'm going to have to put him down."

The line was silent. No breathing at all, like everyone was underwater.

"He's not doing good, well I mean," Sheldon said. "Not doing good at all. He's starting to suffer babe, um, Laura. So I, I called the lady, euthanasia lady and she's coming tomorrow, two p.m."

Laura breathed in. Laura breathed out. "Okay."

"I didn't know if you wanted to see him or say goodbye or whatever."

"I can't."

Sheldon pictured her standing in the window of Lenny's apartment and looking out at the street. She was wearing panties and one of Lenny's giant-ass T-shirts. Lenny lived in a one bedroom right above the Sunset Strip. It was an expensive address for a struggling actor, but not so much for a Molly, ketamine, and mushroom dealer.

"Laura?"

"Yes."

"Please come."

"I can't Sheldon."

"But he, this is your last chance to see him."

Laura took another slow breath. "You say goodbye for me Shel, you were always his favorite."

Sheldon's head got hot and huffed up. "Really? That's it? Just no?"

Silence.

"It's just for, like an hour, or less, a few minutes."

"Sheldon."

"Just one hour Laura, one fucking hour."

"I'm going to hang up now."

"Please don't, please, please, I'm sorry."

Laura didn't hang up.

After a few seconds, Sheldon said, "I'm not asking for you to come back or anything, I, I just want . . . can't we say goodbye to him together?"

Sheldon pictured Lenny shaking his long narrow head or stroking his ratty beard and making a stink face.

"Please Laura."

"I can't Sheldon. That's . . . that's all over. I'm sorry. Give him a kiss for me."

The line went dead.

Sheldon had stared at the phone after Laura hung up and he stared at it now. He thought about calling her again, FaceTiming and making her watch the lady stick a needle into Buddy. Watch the dog that they both had loved die. But Sheldon knew that FaceTime doesn't work like that. You can't make someone pick-up, you can't make them watch.

The doorbell rang. It was a fanfare. When they got the Nest, Laura had wanted to set the chime to something unique and regal, like King Henry the Eighth was making his big entrance. Sheldon had never heard it ring before. The house was deep in the San Fernando Valley, and no one ever came to the door.

He looked at the time. One fifty five.

Sheldon got mad.

Why was the lady early?

Why had they set the doorbell to that stupid fanfare?

Why hadn't he changed it back?

He got madder.

Why did he have to do this?

Why hadn't Laura come for just a few minutes?

Why didn't he and Laura get their pet human?

Why had she run away?

Why hadn't he helped his mom turn his dad so he didn't get that fucking huge bed sore?

Why fucking cancer?

Why fucking, fucking, fucking Lenny?

Sheldon didn't have answers, and the missing pieces were sinkholes inside him. They went deep. He stood up and yanked it open.

"Mr. Shelton?" the lady asked. She was smiling softly.

"What?"

"Mr. Shelton?"

Sheldon took a long breath and let it out. "No."

The lady cocked her head.

"That's not my name."

The lady looked at her paperwork. She had one of those metal document boxes. "Morris Shelton?"

"Sort of. It's Sheldon Morris."

"Oh, I'm sorry."

"That's okay." Sheldon had a wild thought. Maybe this was some kind of black cat in the matrix, maybe because she got his name wrong he didn't have to go through with it, maybe he was going to get some kind of cosmic do-over, for his dad, for Laura, for all of it.

"Does that mean we got a reprieve from the Governor?" Sheldon tried to laugh.

"What?"

"A reprieve." He tried to keep it going, but the lady didn't get it, and Morpheus didn't appear, and his lame joke fell to the ground and lay there.

She said, "I'm sorry, I don't understand. Did you call Angels' Wings?"

The mobile death lady had a soft fleshy face and big brown eyes. Her hair was dyed red. She had a backpack slung over her shoulder and her metal box/clipboard in her hands.

"Yeah. I called." Sheldon and the woman stood facing each other for an awkward moment, then Sheldon said, "Please come in."

The lady stepped inside.

"Would you like to sit down?"

"Thank you." She sat on the couch, and Sheldon sat down on the ground next to Buddy. Buddy thumped his tail, and Sheldon rubbed his ears. She opened up her metal clipboard and took out some papers.

"I have a few questions I have to ask you," she said. Her voice was warm and it warbled a little.

"Sure.

"This is Sonny?"

"Yeah, I mean we called him Buddy, call him Buddy, but yeah."

"How old is Buddy?"

Sheldon said, "He's almost fourteen."

She nodded and smiled. She had a wide mouth, and her smile wasn't in a hurry. She smelled like a hippie, like frankincense or patchouli or something.

She wrote on her form then looked at Sheldon. "I have that there were two owners, you and Laura. Is Laura here?"

Sheldon shook his head.

"Is she coming?"

"No. She and I are divorced."

"Oh, I'm sorry."

"Me too."

The Lady smiled with her eyes, but her lips bent down like she was thinking about something. She got up from the couch. "Is it okay if I sit down here next to him?"

She sat down near Buddy's bum and touched his legs gently.

"Careful," Sheldon said.

The lady looked at him.

"He's had a lot of accidents."

She smiled again. She had nice teeth for a hippie. "Haven't we all, hon. Haven't we all." She kept petting him, and Buddy stopped quivering. "He sure is a big guy."

A wave from the deep rushed Sheldon. "The biggest," he managed, and then the watery hurt overwhelmed him, and he was crying.

Sheldon rubbed Buddy's face and neck fiercely. He bent his head forward, and his tears ran down into Buddy's fur.

The lady kept petting Buddy with her right hand, but she reached her left hand out and put it on Sheldon's shoulder. "He sure seems like a good dog, like a really, really good boy. Like he gets lots and lots of love."

Sheldon was crying freely, fiercely. *Gets love, gets love, got love.* He finally said. "He did. He does."

Buddy was the golden age, the morning sun, the first cup of coffee, possibility and a spring garden, hikes and laughter and sex.

The best there ever was.

The Lady's name was Charlotte. She was strong. After it was over, she slid the body bag under Buddy all by herself.

They sat together on the couch for a good minute, and then she said, "I'm sorry Sheldon, but I'm going to need you to help carry him."

Sheldon was glad that she said him, not it. That she was still talking about Buddy like he was a being not a thing. "Sure," he said.

She put her hand on his forearm. "You did the right thing. It was time, and you let him cross over without any pain, in peace and in love."

"If you're trying to make me cry again, it's not going to work."

"Okay, Mr. Tough Guy." Charlotte laughed.

She had a nice laugh, it was deeper than you'd think.

Charlotte had an old Honda Passport SUV with the first row of rear seats removed. The side door was open, and music played softly from the Honda's stereo.

"Let's set him right here," Charlotte said, and they laid the bag down on a plush dog bed in the back of the Honda.

Charlotte used a fresh Mexican blanket to cover him.

Sheldon felt heat rush to his eyes again. He said, "That's a nice blanket."

Charlotte smiled. "My husband and I used to like to go down the coast to El Sauzal."

"Where?"

"Near Mazatlan, in Baja."

"We used to go to Puerto Nuevo."

"Oh."

"That's where we got them. Our blankets. The one I laid over Buddy." Sheldon wanted to keep talking to Charlotte. He didn't want the talking to end, didn't want the moment after the talking was over to arrive.

"Good Bye Sheldon," Charlotte said, and she put her arms out for a hug.

Sheldon hugged her. The smell of hippie oils was strong. Charlotte closed the doors and climbed into her van. Sheldon walked up the short driveway and stood on the porch.

Charlotte backed into the street.

The Honda made a loud "thunk!" when she switched from reverse into drive, but Charlotte's windows were all open, even though it was cold, and the music was blasting for Buddy and for Sheldon, and it sounded like Joni Mitchell.

Shannon Presby was raised by beatniks and grew up down the street from a Manson crime scene. After high school, he went feral for a time. Later, he was an actor and studied with Stella Adler in NYC, went to law school, clerked for the U.S. Court of Appeals, and became a criminal prosecutor. He's still doing that gig. He is also an MFA student at UCR Palm Desert working on a weird crime novel. His first published short story, *Soundtrack*, appeared this summer in volume 11 of *Kelp Journal*. Shannon likes brown beer, wild places, and words.

MY FAVORITE ANIMAL IS A HARBOR SEAL

Nonfiction by Michele L. Roest

"My Favorite Animal Is a Harbor Seal" was the first-place winner in nonfiction in the 2024 Golden Quill Writing Contest.

When I was a kid growing up in the 1970s, my father, a vertebrate zoologist, taught at the nearby college. On Saturday mornings, I'd go to campus with him, sock-skating the freshly waxed floors in the biological sciences building.

I didn't know what other kids did with their dads, nor did I know that what I did with my dad was unusual. Cleaning animal cages in the labs and responding to calls about wild animals were just part of the normal routine.

People called my dad when they found animals that were injured or had died. We had a big flight cage in our backyard, and when neighbors brought abandoned baby birds to him, he fed them up until they were old enough to fly on their own and released them into the fields behind our house. For animals that had died, he documented what species they were and tried to determine the cause of death. One time, it was a black bear that had been hit by a car, another time, a beautiful pearl-gray dolphin that had washed up on the beach. He kept a record of these findings in order to gather more information about the biodiversity of the central California coastal area where we lived. Once I was old enough to read and write, we'd go together into the field to document a dead animal. He'd hand me the clipboard, instructing me to write the measurements on the data sheet as he called them out.

It was Friday afternoon, the last day of spring break when I was in fourth grade. My dad was teaching, my mom had gone out somewhere, and my older sisters and I were at home. I'd already pestered them enough that they'd closed their doors and told me to go away. I'd read all the books we'd checked out of the library for that week and was aimlessly practicing cartwheels in the front yard when my dad drove up. It was too early for him to be home from work.

"I got a call about a seal on the beach. If you want, you can come along," he said.

I ran to the car.

When we got to the harbormaster's office, my dad identified himself and said someone there had reported a seal. A tall, straight-backed man in a harbor patrol uniform stood up and walked into another office. He walked out carrying what looked like a rolled-up beach towel. Walking right past my father, he dropped the bundle into my arms.

It was a live harbor seal pup, wrapped up in a wet, sandy towel. I looked into the pup's liquid black eyes, and they looked back into mine.

"I thought you were reporting a *dead* seal," Dad said.

A young couple walking the beach had heard the pup's plaintive cries. They picked it up and delivered it to the harbormaster's office. Now, I was holding this baby animal, so human-like that I felt a sense of déjà-vu, as if maybe it *was* a human baby, or maybe I was a seal. The two images, baby and seal, were juxtaposed, swimming in and out of my sight.

It was heavy, almost too heavy, and I didn't trust myself to stand and hold such a precious living thing. What if I dropped it? I would be responsible—I couldn't even allow the thought. I walked outside and sat on the concrete bench, cradling it in my arms. I couldn't stop looking at the huge dark eyes, the silvery speckled fur, the pale whiskers. I could feel the chest rise and fall with every breath. A remnant of the umbilical cord remained, indicating a recent birth within the last couple of days.

I felt an ancient maternal instinct awaken inside of me. I had only one job—to keep this baby safe in my arms. I felt a deep connection to the mothers and big sisters I'd seen holding babies, feeling the same way I did in that moment.

Dad came out of the harbormaster's office. I looked up at him. He looked down at me, and I felt that he, too, had an instinctual sense of his role. It was almost as if we had stopped being who we were and were simply two humans charged with protecting this innocent life entrusted to our care. The moment passed, unacknowledged.

"Your mother will kill me if I let all that sand get in the car," he said. He went back into the harbormaster's office and came out with a large cardboard box for bathroom tissue. He carried the box to the car and put it in the trunk, then took the pup from me and put it in the box. He closed the lid of the trunk. Feeling bereft, I wanted nothing more than to hold it again.

We had a strict dinner curfew at six o'clock. This was before cell phones, so Dad couldn't call my mom and say, "I've got a live harbor seal pup in my car, do you want me to bring it home or take it to campus?" I brushed the sand off my clothes, and we drove home, hearing the pup's loud cries in the trunk.

"Do you think it's going to be okay?" I asked.

"It's fine. Nothing's going to happen to it."

When we got home, Dad opened the trunk and told me to stay with the pup. He went into the house to tell my mother. She came out to have a look.

He picked up the box and brought it into the bathroom. He lifted the pup out and put it in the tub.

"Is it a male or a female?" I asked.

He said it was a male, he could feel the baculum—the penis bone that exists in some mammals, including harbor seals.

"Should we give him a nice warm bath to wash all the sand off?" I asked, thinking of what I would like.

"Cold water only. Think about how cold the ocean is."

I turned the shower spray to cold. The little pup brightened at the feel of the water and swished around in the tub. He seemed to like it!

I could not control my fascination. I felt that he had been given to me, and I was happier than if I'd been given ten birthday presents. I told my mom I didn't need to eat dinner, I would rather stay with the pup. She insisted that I leave the bathroom, put on clean, dry clothes, and join the rest of the family.

As soon as the bathroom door closed, the pup's mournful cries echoed off the walls. I couldn't wait to finish dinner so I could see him again.

"You can't keep it here overnight," I heard my mom say to my dad.

After dinner, Dad put the pup back in the box and drove it up to campus. I was not allowed to come—it was too close to my bedtime. What I didn't realize at the time was that my parents were trying to prevent me from becoming attached to the pup. Too late for that, I was already deeply attached. There was nothing they could have done to prevent it.

The next day was Saturday. I went up to school with my dad. He had put the pup in one of the wire mesh cages outside the lab.

We looked into the cage. The pup looked at us. He seemed happy to see us! I was so happy to see him.

Dad wanted to be there for me when I learned what he knew would be an inevitable and painful lesson, that not all animals survive. But that particular Saturday morning wasn't the day for me to learn that lesson. I wanted to hold the pup again, but my dad said no. He told me not to touch it for any reason—it was a wild animal.

Besides the obvious desire to protect me, his daughter, from the pain of attachment and inevitable loss, my dad also knew that the pup was at risk for imprinting, an instinctive behavior that happens when young animals form an attachment with the first moving thing they see. When a young animal imprints on a human, it can never go back to being with others of its own kind. My father knew that if the pup had any chance of survival, it must not imprint on a human.

"What are we going to feed him?" I asked. He looked at me with a blank face for what seemed like a long time, apparently struggling with some internal decision. Finally, he called his graduate student Claudia, who had studied animal husbandry and livestock care. She asked a friend who took classes in the dairy unit if we could borrow a bottle used for feeding newborn calves. When Claudia arrived, she picked up the pup and weighed him on the scale, then started a journal of everything she did and his responses. While her manner was clinical and unemotional, I was glad for Claudia's involvement. Watching her hold him made it easier for me to remember what it felt like.

Dad called a local veterinarian and got a recipe. He bought sardines sold for fishing bait and heavy whipping cream, combining them in a blender like a milkshake. It wasn't easy getting the concoction into the feeding bottle. It was messy, sticky, and stank like oily fish and spoiled milk. The pup wouldn't take it at first, but eventually he tried a little. My hopes soared.

"Maybe he will live after all," I said. "Do you think we can keep him if he lives?"

Dad shook his head. "If he lives, he'll soon weigh two hundred pounds. We don't have any place to put an animal that size."

He made a call to Marineland of the Pacific and left a message asking them if they wanted the pup. He also had questions about what to feed it. But it was a Saturday, and he knew they wouldn't get the message until Monday.

"Can we name him?" I asked.

"No, we won't have him that long," My enthusiasm was blocked at every turn. It stung, but he was in charge.

I went up to school with him on Sunday too, and Claudia was having some luck feeding the pup. As long as Claudia was there, I felt better. He was so sweet.

On Monday, I went to school. I had to wait until Dad came home from work to hear how the pup was. Still alive.

Marineland didn't get the phone message until Monday afternoon. They called him back and told him to add specific vitamins to the pup's milkshake. They offered to send a special nutrient-rich supplement, but the mail had already gone out. The package wouldn't get in the mail until Tuesday, hopefully to arrive on Wednesday, maybe Thursday. When it arrived, Claudia injected the fluid directly under the skin with a hypodermic needle.

The pup made it all the way to the following Saturday morning. We entered the lab to find Claudia, tears streaming silently down her face, gently stroking the pup's silvery fur. He looked asleep. She said he had died only a few minutes before we got there.

"You can touch him now," Claudia said to me. "It's okay for you to cry."

I was stunned, uncertain of what had happened.

"Are you sure he's dead?"

She said he had taken his last breath ten minutes before we got there. She showed me her entries in the journal she kept. It was all written down, spattered with grease-ringed patches of dried fish mash.

I felt numb, confused. I wasn't allowed to touch or become attached to the seal, but now that he was dead, I was allowed to touch him and cry. My dad's detachment toward the seal felt unnatural, and a part of me wondered if that was how he felt about me. Claudia's warmth and care for the pup were reassuring, but I hadn't been allowed to do what she did. The mixed messages and the confrontation with the dead pup had frozen me emotionally.

"I'm not supposed to cry," I told her. I thought my dad would be proud of me, demonstrating the same detachment he did.

"It's okay," Claudia whispered, still weeping softly. "You can cry over this. You can cry all you want."

This harbor seal pup died long before there were wild animal rescue programs. Harbor seals were rare then; the population was only beginning to recover after the Marine Mammal Protection Act of 1972 banned the shooting of seals. The veterinarians in our town were mostly agricultural, accustomed to treating horses, cows, and sheep.

The well-meaning couple who took the pup from the beach had unwittingly sealed his fate. Harbor seal mothers must leave their pups on the beach while they go into the ocean to find food. This pup's mother was most likely close to shore, eager to return. Sadly ironic, the very act the couple hoped would save his life was the cause of his demise.

Much has changed since then. Marine mammal rescue groups train volunteers to monitor beached marine mammals and prevent people from getting too close. Injured and sick animals are treated by specialized wild animal veterinarians. Animals that die are studied to learn more about their biology and physiology. Those that survive are marked with special tags, indicating their status as rehabilitated animals, and released back into the wild in the hopes they will be able to live out their natural lives, including having offspring, adding to the diversity of the gene pool. Survivors that can't be released become animal ambassadors in zoos and nature centers, providing opportunities for people to see them up close and hear their stories of injury and recovery.

When I grew up, I became a vertebrate zoologist just like my dad. For my master's degree in biology, I studied harbor seals (scientific name: *Phoca vitulina*). I sat on the cliffs looking through my binoculars at the harbor seal mothers with their pups on the beach, their spotted, silvery fur reflecting in the sunlight. Mother harbor seals take good care of their pups, who often head for the water right after they are born. The mother seal will place her body between the pup and the surf, protecting her little one from the impact of the waves. When the mother needs to swim away, her pup rides on her back, holding onto her shoulders with sharp claws. The only time a mother leaves her pup is when she needs to forage for food.

It may come as no surprise that my favorite animal is a harbor seal. Maybe it goes back to my childhood encounter with the little pup that landed in my arms on that spring day. Maybe I've been holding on to him ever since.

Michele Roest was born and raised in San Luis Obispo County. She has Bachelor's and Master's degrees in biology and an MFA in Creative Writing. A field biologist and science educator for more than twenty years, Michele currently teaches in the biology department at California Polytechnic State University. Once a year, she leads a California Naturalist class through Cuesta Community Education. Michele shares her lifelong love for California's biodiversity and the Central Coast at every opportunity.

ANATOMY OF A TRAIN

Poetry by L.I. Henley

"Anatomy of a Train" was the first-place winner in poetry in the 2024 Golden Quill Writing Contest.

Borrow this train, he said, my father himself a freight car
hulking mind aimed headlong, eye fixed on the rails.

Was he talking to me? Sometimes I couldn't tell—
he was always on the horizon, disappearing

into one tunnel or another, surfacing suddenly to bark an order
or teach me, his voice the same for both.

There was no going back. The antique train was coming with me
to school for show-and-tell. If you lose it, or if it breaks…

Have you ever felt a person's presence, looming, making
its own cool shadow, even when you're apart?

Because the person is a train, life-sized and miniature at once?
I landed with a thud, wind knocked out, every time he picked a fight

at the grocery store, in line at the bank, on the street, with a man
he once arrested or wanted to, loaded pistol on his hip, words

exchanged, self-propelled, steam puffing, Borrow this train, and I
had to though I can't tell you what I said about it to my first-grade class.

He'd drilled me on its tiny anatomy: *ballast, blastpipe, buffer,*
the caboose is at the end, the conductor's office, deadman's handle, and I knew

my father was the conductor, the train, maker of the glass
windows the passengers looked out of, and together we were

the junction, splitting off, a fork in the dale. This train, I might
have said, belongs to my father. It's very old and very fragile.

I think I knew the word without being told. It was a word I could feel.
How carefully I carried it home, sweating, trembling as I placed it

back on the mantle, everything glass, the little girl and the father
in the caboose, the father sleeping after a graveyard shift

she mustn't wake him, the air between them fragile.

MEMORY OF AN UNNAMED COLOR

Poetry by L.I. Henley

1. I think the answer has just left me,
that I had it but spilled
the cream, wanting too much at once,
something about the always absent word I reach for
in a divine moment or how there are nothing
but divine moments, beads of cream on the waxy-green
tablecloth, or how all retellings of green
are the crayon's smear of greenness
and not the one you saw as the first camper
awake at dawn, the ferns still lapping azure pools of darkness,
that fragile architecture that keeps me
leaning to look more closely.

2. Disappointment—do you remember?—of taking all ten
of your prized paints and swirling them
together, that unnamed color akin to baby shit,
the lesson of more not equating to better, that love
is an eyedropper and also a firefighter's hose. When it happened,
did you become thrift with color, with love?
With how many names you would cup in prayer?

3. In trying to name the blueness that holds us,
I called it spirit. I called it power. What my friends were told
to call faith, I had no need to name, loving instead
the wildness of uncertainty, sudden wind that shook the cottonwoods,
lifted my skirt and touched me, a blue feeling I didn't own,
was never sure would come back.

4. "It is the best possible sign of a color when nobody who sees it
knows what to call it," said John Ruskin.
When the light came on, I was unable to name the shade of red
our bodies had made. There were so many layers to it.
Neither could the boy who wanted to know
why I'd let it happen. Why didn't I know I was going to bleed
all over his mother's bone-white sheets.

Why didn't I know my body housed an assaulting red,
color provocateur, thief of white.

5. Church hymns, I've read, are full of descriptions of
the heavens, and hardly ever mention the actual color
of the sky. But I was raised a heathen. Sunday mornings
were spent with my father running errands. My favorite
was the hardware store with its bins of silver washers—
flat, toothed, square—the bins of nuts shaped like acorns and castles,
my hands considering what makes a color
warm or cool. The screws with their ovular heads
were decidedly cool, dipped in color I had no word for
and so heard music instead, a one-note "ah" that might beam from a hole
in a veil of cloud, an electric blue maybe or whatever color
electricity makes or every other spark that flies from a welder.

6. The universalists say color is rooted in our biology,
and all I know is that my hand would swim all the way to the bottom
of the bin, my arm buried to the elbow with screws,
my cobalt blood never more at home
than when I stood in aisle ten of the hardware store.
Best still were the paint chips in the interior décor
section: Blue Bell, Rainwater, Chiffon,
Parchment. I felt a deep yearning to eat them,
especially the blues, Robin's Egg dripping from my lips.

7. Ruskin saw the ineffable as sacred. Did it go both ways?
Let me be astonished then, awake too early, alone in a warm
kitchen, tongue lapping the spilled blueness of heavy cream,
let me lean further into an understanding of what light does
and blink—and miss it.

AN OLD FRIEND CALLS TO TELL ME ABOUT THE DEATH OF ANOTHER OLD FRIEND

Poetry by L.I. Henley

"… last December when we spoke
a year ago & has it really been so long?

About Chelsea, I'm sorry &
there's no easy way to tell you

but she passed

she

in a fire, an electrical fire
in the apartment above

her mother's tea shop
She was sleeping

& I'd wanted to tell you
last year when we spoke

but it had been so long since we spoke
& that was too heavy a thing

to tell you just then
not when

you were sick
& not walking—
something to do with wheat?
A disease? You'll have to fill me in.

Her mother … the parents …
they divorced afterward

& I know how much you loved
her brother, sort of an obsession,

right? He was such a man even at seventeen.
The whole family was gorgeous

especially Chelsea, the swimmer,
I'll always remember her swimming

& how strong she was, remember?
Pure muscle, blond hair green from chlorine.

Her sister was the ballet dancer
who lent us tampons all the time.

I'm sorry & you'd just said Chelsea
was the one person from childhood

besides me …
& she was so young

twenty-seven
tragic

a shame

but I have my faith
& I believe Chelsea did as well

& you, L—,
what's going on with you?"

L.I. Henley was born and raised in the Mojave Desert of California. An interdisciplinary artist and writer, her books include *Starshine Road: Poems* (2017 Perugia Press Prize) and the novella-in-verse, *Whole Night Through*. Currently, she's writing personal essays about illness, love, and the Mojave Desert, which have appeared in *Brevity*, *The Southeast Review*, *Southern Humanities Review*, *The Cincinnati Review*, *The Southern Review*, *Fourth Genre*, *The Los Angeles Review*, and *The Mississippi Review*. She teaches English composition at Cal Poly, San Luis Obispo. Visit her at lihenley.com.

THE LILA SEGOVIA SMILE

Fiction by Anne R. Allen

"The Lila Segovia Smile" was the second-place winner in fiction in the 2024 Golden Quill Writing Contest.

Mary Ellen Duggan clutched her Christmas cookie tin and pulled her raggedy suitcase up the leaf-strewn path to Jen's fancy new Portland townhouse. Before she knocked on the door, Mary Ellen pulled a compact from her bag, made sure the make-up still covered her bruises, and practiced her Lila Segovia smile.

She'd been working on that smile ever since she read Lou Bambino's new thriller, *Raven's Eye*. Lila was his best heroine yet. He wrote that "Lila's come-hither smile radiated a self-confidence that came from exquisite bone structure, good hair, and a Beretta in her handbag."

Mary Ellen was a dishwater blond with a flat Irish moon-face, and she didn't own a handgun. But she had a great imagination. She could picture herself becoming somebody like Lila.

Her friend Jen was always reinventing herself —she did it every time she discarded a husband—so why couldn't Mary Ellen do it too? She'd been playing around with a new name: Mariel. She'd started using it as a pen name for the murder mystery she was writing.

Mariel Delgado—a perfect name for her new badass self.

Somebody named Mariel Delgado would not let herself be defined by her luggage. She'd probably have some lethal weapon hidden inside that duct-taped outer pocket. Lila Segovia certainly would.

Mary Ellen couldn't believe she was going to meet Lou Bambino himself—tomorrow! After his book signing at Wordsworth's. He'd answered her email and said he wanted to talk to her. Over coffee. Just her.

Tomorrow was the day everything would change.

But today, she'd have to listen to Jen complain about the Drunken Santa Candy Cane Fudge Bars she'd brought. Jen would say October was too early for Christmas cookies. And she'd remember the recipe called for peppermint schnapps, not vodka and peppermint extract.

Jen had one of those perfect-recall memories. It was like a superpower with her.

Mary Ellen gave a couple of raps with the shiny brass door knocker. Nice place. Jen must have done pretty well in the divorce settlement from that trust-fund hippie.

The door only half-opened.

"Mary Ellen! You're early! I only got off work a half hour ago." Jen peered around the door, still toweling her hair. It was blond now—not a bad color on her.

"Sorry." Mary Ellen tried not to let the chilly welcome discourage her. "I left Kennebec Falls early because I heard it might snow. But it didn't. Clear skies all the way to Portland. It was a nice drive. I'd do it more often if Mike didn't always say he'd miss me too much."

She gave an apologetic smile. She knew Jen had never liked Mike, even back in high school, when he was the big football hero of Kennebec High.

"Where are my manners?" Jen opened the door wide and grabbed Mary Ellen's suitcase.

She rolled it down the hall past a picture-perfect living room and doll-house kitchen—so different from the big, sloppy farmhouse she'd shared with Kipper Van Heusen.

"I put you in my office downstairs because you said you'd hurt your knee in that tumble last month. Are you okay down here? The sofa is a fold-out. It's all made up."

"That's great. Thanks." It was a no-frills room with computer stuff on the desk, but Jen had put a cozy-looking quilt on the fold-out. Mary Ellen had forgotten she'd emailed Jen about her knee.

But as always, Jen always remembered every little detail. That amazing memory.

Which was exactly why Mary Ellen was here.

The pain from the "tumble" still lingered, but the scab was mostly healed. While Jen went upstairs to finish dressing and do her hair, Mary Ellen reapplied the make-up she used to cover the purple marks Mike's fists had left two nights ago. Plus the greenish ones from last week. She didn't want to tell Jen the usual lies about tripping over shoes and walking into doors.

Jen could always see through her—and she didn't understand that divorce was not an option. Mike had promised to arrange a "hunting accident" if Mary Ellen ever told a living soul.

So she kept wearing the make-up and telling lies about how she and Mike were still madly in love.

She changed from her jeans into her best black slacks and the beige silk blouse she'd picked up at the church rummage sale. It was kind of dated, but Mike didn't like her spending money on dress-up clothes. He said it wasn't like she had a real job. Since Sears closed down, she was just the bookkeeper at his garage, and every day was casual Friday.

Jen called from the kitchen with an offer of coffee.

Mary Ellen brought in the cookie tin and sat at the sleek little kitchen table.

Jen gave an eye roll at the elves and holly berries on the cookie tin. "You do know it's not even Halloween yet, don't you?"

"Ay-yup. But I had to bring my famous Drunken Santa Candy Cane Fudge Bars." Mary Ellen opened the tin to show off her carefully arranged chocolate squares with the ground-up candy canes on top. "People always love them no matter the time of year. You were so nice to invite me to your book club dinner. I didn't want to go empty-handed."

Jen rolled her eyes and went to fuss with the coffee. She had one of those new coffee makers that make one slow cup at a time.

"The book club bash is a lot of fun, and you're so booky. I'm happy you could finally come. You'll like these ladies." Jen put another cup into the coffee maker. "I'm taking chicken parmigiana from Lorenzo's. We'll pick it up on the way." The coffee-maker gave a whoosh. "I don't cook anymore unless I have to. I hate having a mess in my kitchen."

Weird. Jen used to be a great cook. But that was with her first husband René. Now she was a bigwig at Coastal Maine Bank, so she could probably afford to buy restaurant food for twenty people, even without whatever she got from Kipper.

Still, Mary Ellen cringed at the expense.

Jen put two steaming cups of coffee on the table along with a pitcher of cream. She chose one of the fudge bars, bit into it, and made a face— the same face she used to make in fifth grade when she got a raisin cookie instead of chocolate chip.

"Oh. You didn't use peppermint schnapps." She put the rest of the fudge bar on her saucer. "Well, I'm supposed to be eating Paleo …."

Time for Mary Ellen to deliver her explanation.

"Mike took the schnapps on his hunting trip. Along with the rest of the booze in the cupboard. Luckily, I know where he hides his spare pint of vodka in the garage, so I could make do with that and peppermint extract. But you know, I worry. The doctor says he should cut back. He has high triglycerides, which is dangerous for the heart. I don't know what I'd do if he had a heart attack."

"All the booze in the cupboard? How many guys are going?"

"Just him. His buddies won't go to his hunting camp anymore. That old place is a wicked mess. I tried to clean it up last summer but only scratched the surface. I found junk his Pop left from when he had the snowmobile, and that had to be twenty years ago."

They sat in awkward silence as Jen stirred cream into her coffee and Mary Ellen ate the biggest fudge bar, to show how yummy they were, even without the schnapps.

"I'm amazed you could come visit," Jen said finally. "How many years have I been inviting you? Mike could finally spare you from the garage?"

"He always closes down at the beginning of bird season for his hunting trip, and I usually use that time to catch up on the accounts, but this year when you told me you were going to be talking about *Raven's Eye*, and going to Lou Bambino's book signing, I decided to take off too. Lou Bambino is my favorite author. And I think I told you I've been doing some writing myself. Not just the church newsletter. I'm working on a mystery. Mike doesn't know."

Jen looked skeptical.

"Mike doesn't know you're writing a novel?"

Mary Ellen shook her head. "He wouldn't want me to get my hopes up. And I didn't tell him about this weekend either, because he gets so jealous, and ..." She lingered on the last word, savoring the dramatic pause. "I happen to have a date to talk to Mr. Bambino tomorrow after his signing."

Jen snorted. "You. Have a date with Lou Bambino. How much vodka did you put in those things?"

"It's not a *date* date. It's a business meeting. Kind of. I wrote him an email. And he wrote back. He asked me to have coffee with him when he's in Portland. He probably didn't know I live three hours away, back in the boonies, but I wasn't going to tell him."

"Lou Bambino answers fan letters? I'll tell the book club!" Jen took another little nibble of her fudge bar. Maybe she forgot she didn't like it.

"What I wrote wasn't exactly a fan letter." Mary Ellen sipped coffee. "It was more like a not-a-fan letter. I hated the ending of *Raven's Eye*. Didn't you? Lila Segovia should not have ended up married. Not to Lazlo anyway. So I wrote Mr. Bambino a piece of my mind. You know how it says in the e-book that 'Mr. Bambino loves to hear from his fans' and there's his email address right there? I was reading it on my phone, so I just hit the link to the address."

"Lila ends up with Lazlo?" Jen put down her coffee cup. "No way! She totally should have hooked up with Jake Stryker."

"You didn't finish the book?" How could a person not finish a book that exciting?

Jen shrugged. "I never have time to finish the book club books these days, with all the work I have to bring home. But I know Lila should have ended up with Jake."

Mary Ellen sighed.

"Nobody can end up with Jake, because he's a loner and a drifter and has to be single for the next Jake Stryker novel. But I think Lila should go on to another adventure like Jake—be a vigilante like him and help other women. She was not made for a lifetime of sappy-ever-after."

"Sappy-ever-after?" Jen gave a big laugh. "That's good. I have to remember that."

"It's what I wrote to Lou Bambino. I was so mad, I even used some nasty words. I have to hear them all the time in the garage, and they kind of slipped out."

"Nasty? I don't believe it. Not Mary Ellen Duggan. And speaking of nasty, do you really not have anything else to wear? Hello? The nineties called. They want their shoulder pads back."

"Mike likes the way I look in this blouse."

"Yeah, well Mike's in the woods drinking peppermint schnapps with the ducks." Jen stood and got her coat. "But we've got an hour, and there's a great little boutique next to Lorenzo's. It's where I got this scarf. What do you say we stop there on the way to dinner? You need to have something nice to wear to meet Lou Bambino. My treat. I'm sure Mike doesn't pay you what you're worth."

Actually, Mike didn't pay anything, even though Mary Ellen ran the whole financial side of the business. She sighed and gave an embarrassed shrug.

"I guess I could use something with a little more color."

"Color? You've been dressing like you want to fade into the woodwork ever since you married that guy. Remember what you used to wear in high school? Miley Cyrus, eat your heart out!"

"But Mike doesn't like me to—"

"Forget Mike, okay?" Jen rolled her eyes, then held up her hands. "I know, I know. He's the love of your life, yadda, yadda, but can you forget him just for this weekend?

The shop next to Lorenzo's was full of flowy bohemian things and beaded jewelry. It smelled like incense and exotic perfume.

"This would look fabulous on you." Jen picked out a brightly embroidered jacket that looked as if it came from someplace you couldn't pronounce.

"Mike would have a fit."

"You're forgetting Mike this weekend, remember? Go try it on." Jen put on her bossy-girl face.

"Try it with these." She handed Mary Ellen some slinky palazzo pants and a low-cut blouse.

Wow. In the dressing room, Mary Ellen looked in the mirror and could hardly believe it was her own self looking back. But it was. Her high school self. All grown up.

Jen came into the dressing room with some chunky silver jewelry: big hoop earrings and a silver pendant shaped like a star. She put the necklace over Mary Ellen's head and held one of the hoops up to her ear.

"You know who you look like now?" she said. "Lila Segovia."

Mary Ellen giggled. "Oh, right. All I need is to dye my hair 'as black as a raven's eye'."

Jen gave a sly smile. "I'll see if my hairdresser can fit you in tomorrow."

"No. I didn't mean for real."

"It will cover up some of that gray." Jen smoothed Mary Ellen's pale hair away from her ears and put on the silver earrings. "Now we've got a party to go to!"

The book club dinner went okay. Except a couple of the ladies turned up their noses when Mary Ellen said she and her husband ran a garage in Kennebec Falls.

But Jen jumped in and said not everybody was lucky enough to be so madly in love with their high school sweetheart they couldn't stand to be away from each other more than a few nights a year.

And everybody loved the fudge bars.

Of course Jen pretended she was the one who had thought up all the stuff about "sappy-ever-after" and how Lila Segovia should have dumped Lazlo.

Mary Ellen ignored the snotty ladies and told the nice ones to call her by her new pen name. Jen said "Mariel Delgado" sounded like somebody's maid, but Mary Ellen didn't care. She had an email account under the name Mariel and that's the name she'd used to write to Lou Bambino.

Now, thanks to Jen, she had the outfit to match.

While the women argued about the book's ending, Mary Ellen turned on her phone and read Mr. Bambino's email again.

"Hi Mariel — I couldn't agree with you more. The ending of *Raven's Eye* sucked. Would you believe I fought with my editor for nearly a month over it?

"In my original ending Lila died in an accident with the motorboat after she poisoned her husband. Jake almost died too, trying to save her in the frigid lake.

"But my editor nixed the death scene. He said the order came down from on high. They wouldn't let me drown Lila because they were in talks about a film … with Jennifer Lopez attached.

"But J-Lo evaporated, the option got dropped, and we had to do something with Lila, so she got stuck with Lazlo. I was hoping for echoes of *Casablanca*. You know, when Ingrid Bergman ends up with Victor Lazlo? But Lila did not deserve a sappy ending. You're damn right.

"Can we talk about it over coffee? I'm doing a signing at Wordsworth's Bookstore in Portland on October 4th. Want to stop by around 5:00? I should be finishing up around then. I'll be the big Italian guy hiding behind the stack of books — Lou."

Mary Ellen took another sip of wine and clicked off her phone. She considered telling everybody that she was going to have coffee with Lou Bambino tomorrow after the book signing—they were all planning to go—but she realized she didn't need to.

There would be plenty of time for surprises tomorrow.

Jen's hairdresser had an opening at three. She was expensive, but Jen said it would be worth it. And it was. When Mary Ellen walked into Wordsworth's at 4:45, her hair was raven's-eye black, cut in a fierce Louise Brooks bob that made her eyes seem bigger and her chin more determined. She couldn't wait to show Jen.

But Jen wasn't at the bookstore. Some of the book club women were still there, standing in line waiting for their autographs. They told her Jen had called and said she had to take care of some emergency at home, and she'd be by later.

They all said they loved Mary Ellen's hair.

Mr. Bambino was indeed a big Italian guy. Tall with a big belly. He looked older and more tired than he did in his photographs, and his smile seemed kind of pasted on.

Mary Ellen got nervous as she waited. She wondered if he'd even remember their "date." He'd sent that email more than a month ago.

One of the ladies introduced Mary Ellen to him, using the name. "Mariel Delgado" sounded so cool when somebody said it out loud.

"Mariel?" Mr. Bambino's eyes widened as he looked up. His smile went from fake to real. "Mariel Delgado, herself?" He took a copy of *Raven's Eye* from the stack and wrote something in it. "Tell the people at the front desk it's paid for. I'm almost done here." He looked at his watch. "They tell me there's a great little Salvadoran place a couple of blocks from here. Do you have time for an early dinner instead of coffee? I love pupusas!"

Mary Ellen had no idea what pupusas were, and she wasn't sure what Salvadoran meant, but she had no doubt Lila Segovia would love it all.

"I think I can fit dinner into my schedule." She took her phone out of her purse and pretended to check her calendar. She had a bunch of texts from Jen, but they could wait.

She told the few book club people who were still there about the dinner plans. The look of envy in their eyes was priceless.

She found a comfy chair in the back and opened the crisp new copy of *Raven's Eye*. No matter how cool e-books were, and how much safer they were to read when Mike was around criticizing everything, there was nothing like the feel of a real, hard-cover book. She opened it and smelled its fresh, inky scent.

On the flyleaf it said:

"For Mariel ... or should I say Lila Segovia? Lou Bambino."

Mary Ellen's heart gave a zing.

The restaurant wasn't much to look at. A step up from a diner with no tablecloths or pictures on the wall like Lorenzo's. At least there was no TV blaring sports, so it was better than anyplace Mike would take her. And the smells were spicy and mouthwatering.

Mr. Bambino said he was going to have a drink called *horchata*, so Mary Ellen said she'd have one too, even though she had no idea what it was.

Then she realized it would be a bad idea to drink anything alcoholic tonight.

"Does it have alcohol? I'd better not ...."

"No. It's a kind of spiced plant milk. It's got seeds and nuts and all kinds of good stuff."

Pupusas turned out to be kind of like a grilled cheese sandwich if you made it with corn bread and put hot sauce and shredded veggies on top. Amazingly good.

So was the *horchata*—sweet and delicious.

Mary Ellen made sure to call him "Mr. Bambino" so the waitress wouldn't get the wrong idea and think they were on a date. She tried to keep her face businesslike.

But that was hard when he started talking. She thought he was going to make more excuses for that lame ending. But he wasn't mad at all.

In fact, he said he loved her ideas for a Lila spin-off.

Like, really loved them.

"You're not even mad at me for what I said about the antifreeze? I should not have said your research was sloppy. That was uncalled for."

Mr. Bambino winced and looked sad.

"Nah. I deserved it. Is that really true? All antifreeze has a bittering agent, so the husband would have known he was drinking poison?"

Mary Ellen nodded. "Ay-yup. Since 2012. It's right there in Wikipedia."

Oh, no. She shouldn't have said "ay-yup." She sounded like a hick.

But he just grinned. "That's a shame for crime writers. Antifreeze is the perfect murder weapon. Tastes like a sweet drink, and it mimics a heart attack. So no autopsy. Plus the killer can be far away, establishing a perfect alibi."

Mary Ellen nodded.

"Yes, but pets like the sweet taste too, and that's the problem. Maine's had the law about adding a bad taste since 2005 and the national law got passed in 2012. So when Lila fed her husband the antifreeze, it should have been some old stuff that had been lying around that mountain cabin. At least since 2012. Not from a bottle she bought new like she did in your book."

Mr. Bambino looked into Mary Ellen's face like he was trying to see some deep secret in there. "Mariel, you're amazing. You've got a fine imagination, and you're a great researcher too." He stabbed an escaping pickled carrot.

Mary Ellen didn't know if he was sad or what.

"Don't feel bad. I loved your book. Lila is my hero. I loved the way she got her husband to take the poisoned peach brandy on his fishing trip even though he didn't care for sweet drinks."

She gave Mr. Bambino a reassuring smile.

"You know, how she kept telling him not to take the brandy because she needed it for a recipe? She knew that would make him take it. That's how guys like that are."

Mr. Bambino took a card out of his wallet and put it on the table next to her plate.

"Contact Anita Snyder at the Snyder Literary Agency. She'll want to see sample chapters."

"Sample chapters?" Mary Ellen had trouble swallowing. This was really happening. Just like she'd imagined it. "You want me to send your agent some chapters of my mystery novel?"

"You have a novel? No. Nothing you've already written."

Her heart deflated.

"I want you to write a new one. I'll give you an outline based on the ideas in your email. We'll be co-authors. James Patterson has dozens of co-authors. It's the new thing."

"You're a much better writer than James Patterson." Mary Ellen had never liked super-violent mysteries.

Mr. Bambino let out a big laugh and patted her hand.

"We're going to get along great, Mariel. I couldn't agree more. But Patterson is a genius at marketing. He's built himself an empire by co-authoring with a bunch of unknown writers. His name on the cover sells the book, and he can come out with four books a month that way. The new writers can establish a name for themselves."

Mary Ellen slowly realized what was happening.

"You don't want me to finish my book?"

"No. I want you to start the Lila novel right now. I'll email you the outline. Anita may even represent your other book if the Lila series does well. She's been hammering me about finding co-authors for at least a year. But I couldn't think of a way it could work. Then I got your gutsy email—like hearing from Lila herself. Boom! Everything fell into place."

"You and I are going to write novels together … about Lila?"

"If you want to."

Mary Ellen's phone chirped. Damn. She'd forgotten to turn it off. Jen must have gotten tired of texting.

"Sorry. I should take this. My friend Jen. She's my ride. She's been texting me all afternoon."

"I can give you a ride," Mr. Bambino said. "If there's a problem …."

Mary Ellen clicked on her phone.

"Why don't you read your damned texts?" Jen's voice sounded all sobby, like she'd been crying. "Where are you?"

"I'm having dinner with Mr. Bambino. What's so important?"

"The Kennebec Falls police were here. It's Mike." Jen took a ragged breath. "He's had a heart attack. Some hunters found him in that shack of his. He'd drunk a whole bottle of that stupid peppermint schnapps and …." Jen blew her nose. "It looks as if he's been dead since early last night. All that time we were shopping and sipping chardonnay at the book club dinner, Mike was …." She let out a deep sigh. "The police wanted to know where you were all that time, so I told them, chapter and verse …."

Mary Ellen was sure Jen had described every minute of her alibi. Jen had one of those memories.

Mary Ellen took another sip of her *horchata* and smiled at Mr. Bambino. He was talking to the waiter, but he kept looking at her, like she was somebody special.

Jen was really turning on the waterworks.

"Oh, Mary Ellen, I feel so guilty." Jen blew her nose. "I'm the one who told you to forget about Mike this weekend, and now I feel so awful. They want you to go back tomorrow to identify the body. I'll drive you to Kennebec Falls. You shouldn't have to do it alone. This is going to be such a tough time for you."

"It sounds as if you've been drinking, Jen. Are you all right?"

"Oh my God. You're in shock, Mary Ellen. You're not hearing me. Your husband is dead. He had a heart attack. You said he had high triglycerides …."

"Mr. Bambino says he'll drive me back to your condo. We can talk then."

Mary Ellen clicked off her phone and gave a silent prayer of thanks to her late father-in-law for that ancient antifreeze she'd found at the hunting camp.

She drained the last of her *horchata*. It was good to know Mr. Bambino liked sweet drinks. She was going to remember that. Even if she didn't have a memory as good as Jen's.

Mary Ellen stood and gave Mr. Bambino her Lila Segovia smile.

Anne R. Allen has been a member of Nightwriters for 28 years. She's an award-winning blogger and the author of 15 books, including the bestselling Camilla Randall Mysteries. Her blogging guide, *The Author Blog: Easy Blogging for Busy Authors*, was named one of the "Best Blogging Books of All Time" by Book Authority.

MY WRINKLED BRAIN

Nonfiction by Rusty Evans

"My Wrinkled Brain" was the second-place winner in nonfiction in the 2024 Golden Quill Writing Contest.

Lately, I've had this suspicion my brain is wearing out. I'm not angry about it. I'm pretty sure I anticipated it. I don't have any memories of thinking about it much up until now. Maybe I put it out of my head, hoping it wouldn't happen. But now, I wonder, did I do that deliberately, or did the expectation wander off on its own? I don't remember, and there lies the problem. The state I'm in is often one of confusion of late. So far, at least, it's been a vacation getaway, not a place I'd call my permanent home.

I've had a good run with this brain. It helped me get into college many years ago, leading me to non-homework classes. It allowed me to cram enough information during last-minute, amphetamine-fueled nights to pass tests. Meanwhile, some of its sections were never fully developed, like the ones that control the motivation to do things like "make the bed" or "hang up clothes." My brain helped me accept this by reassuring me, "Nobody's perfect."

Indeed, I don't want to piss it off at this point in my life. As a white-haired male in the dusk years of his life, I will need all of it, so I'm choosing to stay on friendly terms. I don't need some A.I. wannabe in my head with an agenda.

This self-examination began after I came across an article (online post) discussing the deterioration of our mind and physical brain while still alive. I decided, right then and there: This is happening to me! Why not? Very few of my decisions over the years were made with its preservation in mind. For instance, I used to play tackle football without a helmet, something most medical professionals would agree might not be the best activity for a teenage head. Growing up, no one ever told me that French fries and Orange Crush weren't part of a brain-healthy diet. The importance of exercise and sleep for maintaining future cognitive fitness should have been clarified. But I won't be all bitter and angry over something that happened so long ago. That isn't a sensible response to something somewhat out of my control. (I read that on the internet, too.)

What precisely is going on, or not going on, in that brain of mind to cause concern? Well, come to find out, the human brain shrinks as we age. When we were growing up, we were taught that we only use ten percent of our brains and that ninety percent of it is left unused. However, studies now show that this is a misconception. While we may use only about ten percent of our brains at any moment, we use nearly all of our brains at different times. Neuroscientists have researched this and have proven this point despite no apparent good reason for them to do so.

Another issue is something called cerebral atrophy. This is the fancy title for the condition caused by the loss of brain cells. Most cells will regenerate, so losing a few is no big deal. Except, when we were in school, brain cells were the exception. Back then, if you killed them with drugs, for instance, they wouldn't be coming back. These same neuroscientists, probably trying to make up for taking our excess unused brain mass away, have decided that brain cells regenerate after all. Growing up might have been much more enjoyable had we had the correct information.

One positive finding was that seniors, if given the opportunity, can learn a new task and do it as well as someone younger. It's simply a matter of giving us enough time to get it done. Of course, that is something we have less of left. And if there are printed directions, the font size would have to be big enough to read, so it might take a grove of trees to make the paper necessary. But if the challenge is simple enough and doesn't require patience, dexterity, or decent vision, there is no limit to what we older people can do!

I caution older Americans against running for political office, however. Seniors have been known to win elections, which gives them a job that requires quick thinking on their feet. I know I can't even stand that long, to begin with. And being upright can cause gravity to slow blood pumping to our brains, making it less efficient. That's not science; that's common sense.

Our cerebral cortex, the brain's outer layer, also changes as we age. Seniors expect their hair to get gray and their skin to become wrinkled, but this isn't what happens with our brains. After all, there's already gray matter there, and the surface of the cerebral cortex is wrinkled anyway. It gets thin, but unlike with our bodies, getting thinner as the years go by is not good. This change in structure slows down the cognitive synapses. This could mean we might be unable to solve complex trigonometric problems and quadratic equations as they arise. But rest assured, most of us can survive with little change in our daily routine.

There are four areas most affected by the maturing adult brain: recall, multi-tasking, learning, and processing. Each of these results in different symptoms, which are essential to recognize. Here are some examples, for instance, of what one might encounter on a trip to the grocery store:

1. If you're leaving for Albertson's, you can't find your keys after locking the house and getting into your car. You go back into your home, look in all the usual spots, decide they must be in the car, go back out, lock the door, get back into the —car—and there you find them in your hand. *Recall* is remembering you can't lock your house without keys. But now you can't find your sunglasses ….

2. So, on your way to the store, you keep one eye on the road while the other searches the floor for your Ray-Bans. You answer a call from India, use your knees to steer, and then reach under the seat with your free hand. Without warning, your sunglasses drop onto your lap because someone has stuck them on your head. This is *multitasking*, something law enforcement prefers you not to do while driving at any age.

3. While shopping, you notice a lot of discounts via "digital coupons." You've never used them. You ask a clerk, who instructs you to go to the grocery store website on your phone to download them. After mixing up the letters, you end up in a chatroom with a three-legged dominatrix on a North Korean porn site. You ask the clerk for help again, but she gasps and drops your phone in the dairy case. This is when there isn't enough time for your older brain to start *learning* something new.

4. Usually, you play a game with yourself and try to add up the prices while they're being scanned to see how close you get to the final total. This time, the first item is a pound of bacon for $13.99. The aging brain stares at the package, now in your grocery bag. The clerk continues to check items, but your brain is stuck in a *processing loop*. You swipe your card, averting your eyes from the final tally.

Given severe brain disorders and disabilities are no joke, we need solutions sooner rather than later for diseases like Alzheimer's, Parkinson's, and ALS. The aging brain, however, is not an illness, just part of a maturing life. We should rejoice after making it to this stage; the brain has evolved into something better suited for life going forward. Do not worry; your mind can continue to thrive and, at the same time, stay firmly in the gutter.

Indeed, there will be seniors who make it to their golden years but will need help remembering what made them so golden. But a slower brain may not be all bad for many of us. Our body compensates for aging by giving us snail-like reactions, and with everything now in slow motion, we may never even notice that much has changed.

I've decided to be okay with my brain being a little more tired. It's worked hard at hardly working for me through the years. We've been inseparable from birth, and I don't think either would do very well without the other. We'll need each other to muddle and navigate through our senior years together.

Originally from the great town of Tulare in the San Joaquin Valley, **Rusty Evans** came to the Central Coast in 1979 after leaving Fresno State, where he studied history. He was determined to make his life here, and he did so by succeeding in car sales until his retirement in 2022. His wife, Stacy, is a retired Public Health Microbiologist. Rusty has published bad country western songs and meant-to-be humorous essays over the years and has a half-written mystery novel somewhere on his hard drive. He is chancellor of Baywood State, a fake school with a website selling real T-shirts.

GAME TIME

Poetry by Misty Wycoff

"Game Time" was the second-place winner in fiction in the 2024 Golden Quill Writing Contest.

I often wake with the first line of a poem
floating around me, calling,
asking if I will come out to play.

Just like the neighbor kid
who sat on the stoop waiting,
no words beyond the nod or the "Hey,"
spoken with our eyes sweeping ahead.

A long day's possibilities beckon
to the game that we would make,
after walking to the empty field,
trusting something unspoken,
watching the stray cat climb
the right field fence,
relying on the glove
that I haven't taken off all morning,
or that beat up ball
lying behind the backstop.

Pace quickens as we enter the grounds,
checking the outfield for intruders
kicking the sweet soft dust underfoot
playing the silence as it bounced off
the much larger imagined roar
as we step on the ball field.

With minds drenched in knowing
how sweet the ball would feel
smacking into the back of the glove,
or hearing the swinging bat clack,

or feeling the loping run and tagging up,
getting ourselves home.

Like that, as I left the bed,
I moved towards the blank page
carrying something in my pocket
looking for a game.

EXPLORATION

Poetry by Misty Wycoff

A child fell to the ground,
stepping instead into the veil
of gravity,
his hand ripping through the portal
and wounding itself.
A small tear, a bit of blood, a pinprick,
a new experience
this wound.

Then, this little boy
held his whole arm up
as if broken, flat out in front of him,
bracing it below the elbow,
the scraped hand splayed ahead of him,
upward, needing someone to see
the innocence taken.

During the walk home
he kept the posture,
holding the arm like a prize,
like something now separate from himself,
closer now to his chest,
hand still open to the sky,
honored and anticipating the cure.

He was beginning to probe,
testing the many pathways
the routes to soften and palliate the damage,
finding a practice that will assuage
and bring ease to the many lacerations and losses
that life will put before him.

Like the God Aesclepius
who found that healing
was intrinsically bound

to the wound itself
his body knows that the small gash
the one that has pierced his veil of invincibility
is now the God itself,
the thing that will bring him closer to his core,
his real boy,
the one who lives beneath all the others.

A NEW TUNE

Poetry by Misty Wycoff

I imagine myself in a hallway,
outside a music room with a piano,
hearing but not seeing
a small girl beating out the high notes
both hands in flight.
The plunking, clinking of the black and whites
filter into the day, surround me,
pairing themselves
with my heart's new rhythm.

Weeks ago, a surgeon's wire found its way
up inside my ventricular chamber,
testing, burning little bits of me
forcing the impulses to find
a better pathway.
And now, a knowing,
a felt shadow, a trace of a presence.
Somehow like that time, decades ago,
when I came home from the movies,
to my house, which had been robbed
and the hair on my neck was upright.

It wasn't what was lost,
but the intrusion
that left its mark.
In the space that holds my heart,
there is now something else.
A memory perhaps,
of a girl, touching a piano,
the long wires setting something free.
I see her skirted legs swinging
beneath the dark piano bench
laying down the beat.

This new music has settled with me,
escaping the keyboard,
passages in the air
both found and lost,
all while she, determinedly,
tries to find the newest tune.

Born to a world of high grass, crawdad creeks, and sharecropper orchard houses, **Misty Wycoff**'s early life was often spent in solitude, perched in the low branches of an old cypress tree, communing with the ranch dogs and wild animals, or barefoot, clamming the mudflats around Bodega Bay California. After nearly twenty years in Los Osos, she finds a deep resonance here to the land of her upbringing. Her first book *High Rain* came out in 2019, and she is currently editing her eighth book, *Dwelling*, which should be in local bookstores by early 2025. Contact through website is: bmistywycoff.com.

THE MARY TAFT MYSTERY

Fiction by Kevin Carver

The first thing you need to know is that Momma changed the world. This was back when America was young, in the 1980s. We pumped our gasoline before we paid for it. You believe that? It's true. Total honor system. Momma'd grip the hose handle with a polite wave to whichever attendant patrolled nearby with a half-ashed cigarette and a broom. She'd casually lean against her 1973 Mercury Marquis, chipped and dented, road-gray except for a replaced passenger door that was all green; she'd wait a short eternity for the click, holster the thing, fall into her seat, wink at me, the panicky child in her rear-view mirror, before cranking the keys and slamming the pedal. Our balding tires screeched to the interstate like a rat without its tail. Occasionally she neglected the hose altogether, either by accident or on purpose, I never knew, and in those moments the Marquis appeared to grow a tail that flapped wild and alive on the sparky highway. She had done it one too many times, Momma later explained to me, and next thing you know: *Pre-Pay Only*. What total bullshit, she liked to say.

You wouldn't know it, being so young and clean, but we also lived in a world that wrote checks. You ever write a check? Yeah I didn't think so. Every day we did, little paper promises at the grocery store, the hardware store. In AutoZone, I don't know. It didn't matter if we didn't have the dough, not really. This was an IOU, Momma explained to me, and it would all figure itself out. What happened? Yeah, exactly. You get it. This guy gets it. Momma wrote one too many IOUs. Now you see her everywhere, don't you, her laminated legacy reading *No Checks*.

We were once a nation without IDs. Bet you didn't know that. America, from sea to shining sea, from the lakes of Tennessee to the hills of Texas, or whatever. People used to shake hands. That was good enough. "Remember that tight ass at your school who didn't let me pick you up? Had to drag you out of there screaming," she once told me in between drags of her Basic Filters, the kind from the red and white box. She held her cigarette to her chest like a cross. What total bullshit, she chanted, casually dismissing a traumatic episode from my childhood.

Momma died full of secrets and stories, an excuse for each debt and an escape from every debtor. People still look for her, even now, five years later.

Towards the end she became what can only be described as Proper Crazy. Momma had always been manic and unstable, depressed, you know, but in her final years she progressed into paranoia and schizophrenia. The ugly kind. She wore safety glasses in public. She lined her jackets and shoes with aluminum foil. *They* were trying to kill her with electricity, she told me. Only twice was I brave enough to ask who *they* were, scratching the logic, but her eyes would rove onto some new fantasy, some new buzz, a conspiracy of victims and villains.

My house was where she lived her final year, and it was her first settled residence in decades. Forget what you're thinking. I can see it in your eyes. This wasn't some magical and sentimental year of burying hatchets or singing showtunes. Momma moved in like a tornado and left much in the same way. It was a tough year that ended tough.

Though the world quickly moved on from Momma, my thoughts were never far from her. One reason is I still received Momma's mail. Fliers and coupons, collection notices, letters from lost lovers. *Junk mail.* It grew like mold on my kitchen table. What can I say? You get to a point in your life where you just stop keeping up, and your house reflects the cluttered chaos of your brain. Anyway, debt collectors loved my address because they finally had one with which they could pursue her. Unfortunately for them, Momma fled this mortal gas station. You could say evading was her life's work and that she died doing what she loved. Ha, I guess you really could say that. I hate it when I snort.

So this mess, the one I'm telling you about today, started eight months ago, long after Momma had passed. I opened my mailbox and found the typical stuff, more of what I just explained. Junk mail for me, some for Momma. There was a bill for me and then there was a letter. It wasn't for me, and it wasn't for Momma. It was addressed to my home, to a stranger, someone named Mary Taft. My name's not Mary Taft, not even close.

I brought the letter inside, took it to my kitchen bar counter, one of the few cleared surfaces left, brushed away those pesky cracker crumbs, and stared at the envelope for God knows how long. I grabbed a dead pen. I searched for more pens. This whole process took, I don't know, thirty minutes or so. Eventually, I found a living pen and proudly wrote, *Not At This Address.* I journeyed back to the curb, returned the letter to my mailbox, and, exhausted, flipped the flag like an early settler.

Like Tom Cruise in that one movie about the settlers. You know the one. Nicole Kidman's in it. The Oklahoma settlers. Oh I'll think of it.

The next day, when I checked the mailbox everything was normal, but the day after that, guess what happened? Another letter for Mary Taft! My home address, again! I brought the letter inside, again! Crossed it out, again! Explained *why* on the envelope, again! Rejected it back to the mailbox, again!

Frustrating, I thought. *Annoying.*

The next day was Sunday then the day after that a federal holiday. So it was Tuesday before I finally had mail again. This time I brought the pen with me to the curb and would not bother with that whole exercise back and forth, because I just assumed more Mary Taft mail was in my future. I'm no dummy, okay? Bring your umbrella if it's raining shit, Momma said to me once. This time it wasn't a letter. It was an official notice from the Post Office. *Notice of Changed Address for Mary Taft.* I studied it from the curb. I compared the address on my home to the address on the paper, holding it in the air. I did this four or five times. "Huh," I finally said.

Mistakes were made. Someone screws up and then *you* have to pay for it. This was not the first nor I'm sure would it be the last fat-finger typo to inconvenience my life.

Was I angry? No, to be completely honest. It can be thrilling to have a legitimate complaint, for being that person representing unquestionable rightness.

I wanted to really make a show of it too: *Look and see, feel the damage of your mistakes! I have a cane, and you make me come all the way down here? My bad knees?*

I spent the day thinking all about it. All the different speeches I would give depending on the type of person I found at the counter. This mania, I guess you could call it that, lasted into the evening and then into night where sleep eluded me. I finally slept around three o'clock in the morning, watching reruns on TV Land where families with normal houses and proper lives reacted to inconvenient plots with comical high jinks in black and white.

I awoke to a crash so loud I thought the world was ending.

I rubbed my head, assuming it was a nightmare, and then heard it again. *CLANG. CLUNG. BOOM. PSHHHH.* The boom banged again. Something horrendous scraped something stubborn. My first thought was that my house was collapsing but thankfully my house wasn't collapsing. The racket nearly gave me a heart attack.

Not to mention, geez, it was early, and I had been up all night.

So I grabbed my robe, stuffed my feet into mismatching slippers, and marched to my living room window angrier than I might have ever been. I looked and there it was, a shipping container in my driveway. "PODS" was written on its side. A truck with a large trailer was unloading it, the driver winding up the last of his straps.

"Excuse me," I said through the window. I started yelling. I tapped the glass like a nervous cat. Unbothered, the driver jumped into his truck. I realized I had to get out there. I fumbled through the door and ran out into my driveway. The truck left me behind in a hurry, looking rather carefree and burdenless. I stood there, yes yes yes, like a dingbat in the early morning mist, incredulous, okay? Honestly a little unkempt.

I stared at this shipping container, if you really can believe it, filling up my whole goddamn driveway.

You know those old alien-invasion creature features they play on TCM in October? That's what it was like when the pod arrived: unannounced and sudden, like a saucer.

I got dressed. I paced around my house for an hour. I guzzled Mr. Coffee's finest as I looked upon my new travesty, trying to blink it out of existence.

I wondered what the hell was inside it.

Surely nothing nefarious. Furniture and clothing. Lamps. Trinkets. How could I know? It was locked and Mary Taft had the key. I contemplated this mess I found myself in and concluded there were likely three reasonable scenarios that would explain what was happening.

First Reasonable Scenario: I was dead. I had died.

The most fantastical option is sometimes the simplest. You know, Occam's shaver. Maybe this is how you find out you're dead. You think you're alive and pissing and then someday a stranger moves into your home, like the ghosts in *Beetlejuice*. I found that old VHS tape and popped it into my VCR. Google it and you'll see what I mean. The machine still worked. Some dancing squiggles on the screen, you know, damage to the tape, but the opening credits hit me like comfort food, and I watched the movie twice, once in awe and then again in tears. I thought I better get up and get dressed to figure out if I was really dead or not.

In *Beetlejuice*, if you've seen it, these poor ghosts are trapped in their home; when they leave they find only sandworms in a wasteland. Me: I was able to freely leave my home, no problem, no sandworms. I already mentioned all my trips to the mailbox. But when was the last time I walked past my mailbox? I suddenly realized I hadn't been to the grocery store in months. When was the last time I had eaten anything?

Here's the truth: I clasped onto my mailbox for about twenty minutes, stretching my foot as far as it would go, sweating, shaking, aching, frightened, pausing to wave at walking neighbors, pretending to fix the mailbox without any tools, and finally, you know, after a few false starts and a soldier's courage, I let go. One step, two steps, further and further down my street I pranced like a possessed ostrich. My neighbors must have had quite the show, but fuck them.

Okay, listen, people who live alone are prone to wild thoughts and flights of fancy and that's all it was. To be sure though, I drove down to Wegmans and chatted with a cashier. She looked right at me and spoke words. I asked her if I looked okay and she said I looked healthy, which wasn't exactly what I had asked, but that was fine. I then asked her if I could write a check, and she apologized and said no. She pointed to the sign. No problem, I assured her. Thank you.

Second Reasonable Scenario: the pod was a trap.

The letters were fake. The pod was empty. There was no Mary Taft.

What they wanted me to do was open the letters (more had arrived in the days since the pod invaded my driveway), and these letters would hold instructions. The second you open it they get you. They accuse you of fraud. Then I would have to pay some egregious amount of money that I of course did not have.

Momma would have loved all this.

Or maybe not. Maybe she would have been frightened stiff and used it as an excuse to leave in the middle of the night, as she often did throughout her nomadic and troubled life.

I no longer marked Mary Taft's letters for return.

I kept them on my kitchen counter in a neat little pile. It would make sense to open one, I finally concluded. I could always reseal it, like they do in those old spy TV shows, and deny, deny, deny. I grabbed an envelope. It was forest green and looked like a holiday card. I held it to the light. This did not help, but it made me feel productive. Sure, the prospect of partaking in everyday espionage excited me. I admit it. I put on a teapot. I waited for the steam. I held the card over the steam, high above so it wouldn't permanently damage the paper, and patiently waited for the seal to *unlick*. It took too long, so I ripped it open and hungrily consumed its contents. It was a card, a birthday card with balloons on the cover. *Just Wanted To 'Pop' By And Say Happy Birthday*, it read. On the inside I found, "Happy Birthday, Mary," written with lazy blue ink and then,

"PS: SO excited for you!" I dropped the card and hurried to the sink where I threw up.

Like you've never made a mistake? You will. Trust me, you will.

It wasn't just that I defiled a poor stranger's mail, some innocent birthday card. What made me sick was that I could feel the paranoia infecting me. I was suspicious of a *they*. Was Momma's illness in me too, sprouting like a dormant seed? I hurriedly closed my curtains. I made some tea. *The Beverly Hillbillies* was on.

Third Reasonable Scenario: Mary Taft was a real person, a nice person.

She was someone you wanted to know. People sent her cards on her birthday even though she was an adult. This meant she was good at sustaining relationships. Salt of the earth, Mary was. She was divorced young and had to pull herself up by her bootstraps. No kids. She lived alone, like me. But Mary's story was not a sad one. She was a successful woman, a professional individual navigating the challenging and choppy Seas of Life. She made a mistake, okay? She wrote down the wrong address. She's busy and overwhelmed. Maybe she had a kid after all. She was frazzled. Why wouldn't she be? A working single mother. Her kid should be so lucky. The mistake snowballed. She gave the wrong address to the Post Office. She gave it to the container company. She gave it to her family and friends. Any day now, I suddenly realized, Mary Taft would show up at her incorrect address, which was also my address.

I frantically started to clean.

The day Mary Taft arrived was, oddly enough, Momma's birthday. I had a feeling this would happen. I could not tell you why or what it meant, but there you go. I had cleaned up and dressed to the nines. I was all nerves and hit the toilet four or five times before an unassuming blue sedan pulled up to my curb. She stepped out of the backseat and there she was, Mary Taft. Early thirties, neither skinny nor fat, neither tall nor short, a brunette with long hair pulled tightly back. She wore a business skirt with a blazer. High heels. Her legs looked professional. I could not tell you if this was how I had envisioned her or not. The mock sketch I drew of her in my mind fizzled as soon as the real one arrived.

The car was an Uber, or something like that. Her driver helped her retrieve her airline roller bag out of the trunk. He waved and then drove away. Dignified-like, she stood at the curb surveying my property, looking like a realtor standing there. I made a mental note to remember to tell her that. Mary Taft walked to the pod, searched for a key on her person, found it in her cute green pebbled-leather purse, and unlocked it. She rolled up the container door and revealed its contents, which were mostly tools and cleaning supplies.

"Huh," I said.

It was at this point that I realized she was staring at me. I panicked. Have you ever really panicked? I mean sincerely. People say they panic, but they have no idea what they're talking about. Imagine the air in this room's suddenly toxic but you have to keep breathing it anyway. Imagine learning your blood is poisoned and there's nothing you can do to keep your heart from pumping it into your brain. It's like the world is ending and your shoes are untied. I felt warm, is what I mean. I had planned to stand at the front door with a friendly wave, but I skiffed it up. What a wretched first impression. I did not want to be a snoop, you know, yet here I was peeking into her steel closet like some brat kid through a keyhole. I cursed. I realized I was scowling, so I smiled. It was a forced smile with too much teeth and an open mouth. I waved. I nailed the wave, I think. Not too strong, not too weak. Not too high, not too low.

Mary Taft did not wave back.

In fact, she dropped her purse and threw her airport roller to the ground and marched to my front door, trying the knob, and then began furiously pounding on the door with her fist. Everything was suddenly very wrong. Incredibly wrong. I listened to her pound on the door as I slowly backed into a closet. *BANG. BANG. BANG. POUND. POUND. POUND.* I heard her curse in a really nasty way, more inventively than you would think. *BANG. BANG. BANG. POUND. POUND. POUND.* She must have walked over to where she threw her purse. I heard what sounded like rustling and shifting papers.

"Jamie Tabbelton?" she asked, practically yelling. *Oh sure*, I thought, *let's bring the neighbors into this.* She repeated my name, angrier and louder, and then demanded, "Answer or I call the cops."

"I'm calling the cops, okay. It's me who's calling the cops." I felt both brave and weak for yelling it. The truth was that I still wanted to fix the situation. Mary Taft and I could still be friends. This was the wrong foot by a mile. The wrong leg, the wrong arm. The wrong house. Broom raised in my hand like a witch, I slowly left my closet, inching forward toward the locked front door that still divided us.

"Jamie Tabbelton, is that you?"

"Yes!" I yelled back. After a beat I added, "Happy birthday."

It just popped into my head.

"Fucking bullshit," I heard her say. She stomped off, her heels stabbing the concrete as if she were hunting ants. I ran to the living room window and watched her slam the pod shut. She locked it. She shook her head the whole time, muttering. I think I heard her laugh and say words like *unbelievable* and *fantastic*. She grabbed her bags and left the property, freely and without fear, and I never saw her again.

They told me Mary Taft had bought my home.

Paul, a plain-clothed twenty-something college graduate with red ears from the county explained it to me. He said I hadn't paid my property taxes in five years. He said something about tax deeds. He said they had sent me letters. He said a surveyor came to my house and appraised it, that I had signed papers. "Here, look."

I told him I thought the surveyor was from the insurance company. The excuse felt flimsy in the light of day and in full knowledge of all the events, but it was true. I also tried to remember if I had forgotten to pay my home insurance.

"The county made an error," Paul added. He said they forgot to send someone out here to tape off the house and make sure I had vacated the property. "Consider this an official notice: the county is giving you thirty days from today. After that time Ms. Taft will assume the property."

"What total bullshit," I said.

"Regardless," Paul continued while collecting copies of the papers he had me sign and putting them into a folder so I could later not read them, "I would get your affairs in order. Like I said, you have thirty days." Paul daintily shook my hand and left. I sat and studied the ceiling for a little while, and then I watched *Green Acres*. It was a good one.

Maybe it would have been easier if I really were dead. I think I would have preferred to haunt Mary Taft. No, really. She would have eventually run out of the house screaming. It would be night, and it would be raining.

Then I realized Mary Taft would never live in my home. She was a flipper, see? She wanted my house's bones so she could dress them up like a pimp and put them on the corner to slow passing traffic. It's only been six months and the For Sale sign has already been planted like— oh! *Far and Away*, that's the name of the movie, the settlers from Oklahoma.

So look, I tell all of this to you now because it has finally occurred to me that I was scammed out of my home. Scammed! These people were not real people. You see that, don't you? They were crooks, actors. They were the *they* Momma had been warning me about.

Who takes a person's home? You wouldn't do that.

I want to sue them. That's why I'm here. Sue, isn't that funny. Momma's name was Sue.

All she left me were these safety glasses.

Kevin Carver is a writer, musician, and digital marketer from Oceano, California. A graduate of the creative writing program at the University of Rochester, New York, Kevin's work has appeared in multiple publications, including *585 Magazine, Spokane + Coeur d'Alene Living, Behind the Setlist, The Inlander, CITY, Reflections, Trestle Creek Review,* and more. Additionally, he produced two one-act plays and recently self-published a marketing guide for musicians. His debut fantasy novel, *The Forbidden Parallel,* will be published in 2025 by Provender Press. Learn more about Kevin online at kevincarver.com.

THE STOIC PARENT

Nonfiction by T.K. Schuberth

"The Stoic Parent" received an Honorable Mention in the 2024 Golden Quill Writing Contest.

> *Early on in the [Covid] crisis, I picked up Marcus Aurelius and for the first time in my life read his* Meditations *not as an academic exercise, nor in pursuit of pleasure, but with the same attitude I bring to the instructions for a flat-pack table—I was in need of practical assistance.*

> —Zadie Smith, *Intimations*

Ancient Stoics like Marcus Aurelius didn't just write about philosophy. They engaged in mental exercises to force themselves to live in the moment. The practice I recall most vividly is of a man holding his newborn and imagining the baby as dead. When I first read the Stoics, I didn't have children and could intellectually understand the point. Because we are so worried about what might happen, we never enjoy the person in front of us. We don't live in the moment.

The fucking Stoics never had to wait for follow-up scans or biopsy results for their teenager.

People often think my fourteen-year-old is sixteen if not eighteen. He grew ten inches and three shoe sizes during Covid. After his first vaccination shot, a lump formed in his neck. When the doctor looked at my history, she ordered a scan—for the next day.

My history.

I'm used to discussing "my history" in examination rooms with posters of rolling hills and pamphlets about free wig Fridays. The medical profession tries, but when I was diagnosed with breast cancer at forty-one, I didn't want a yoga class. Statistics and a little humor were what I craved.

An MRI reveals my son is fine. An inflamed lymph node from the vaccine. My history isn't in him—yet.

My mother's first diagnosis came when I was fourteen. Ovarian cancer. Surgery, chemo, remission. My senior year of high school, I went to the gynecologist for the first time. A week later, a grapefruit-sized cyst was removed from my ovary. Two weeks after that, I learned it was benign. I went to college. My mother got breast cancer. Two years later, the doctors told us she had lung cancer. She didn't. She had a bacterial superbug—likely picked up in the hospital during her other surgeries. What a relief.

It's now Wednesday. My son doesn't want to miss math class, but his ankle has been bothering him all week. It's swollen. When he was younger, he was such a Stoic that by the time he told us his throat hurt, he usually had a full-blown ear infection or pneumonia. So when he asks for Advil two days in a row, I make an appointment.

In the pediatric waiting area, a toddler screams while her mother ignores her; an exhausted dad rocks a baby; and my son, in his David Bowie T-shirt and size eleven shoes, looks at his phone.

After twenty minutes, they call our name.

The exam room is cheery, the white walls broken up by green panels and a menagerie of cut-out decals. A bird, a bunny, a chicken, and what appears to be a mouse, although his size relative to the other animals makes him look more like a rat. A sign above the exam table, in English and Spanish, reminds parents not to leave children unattended because they could fall. My son sits on the table, his feet flat on the floor.

We have been waiting half an hour, and my throat is dry. The air quality is poor. For the past four days, a fire in the Columbia Gorge has left a haze over Portland. Kids are kept in from lunch. Sporting events are canceled.

The nurse takes my son's vitals. Mercifully, she is wearing plain purple scrubs. No little hearts or cartoon characters. She asks questions off a computer screen. How long has your ankle been swelling? A few days. Was there an injury? No. When does it hurt? The morning.

"It hurts more in the morning than at night?"

"Yes."

"Now you've got me interested," she says.

When she leaves, my son comments about all the box-checking. From his perch, he could see her screen and the decision trees produced by each answer she clicked. I say something about evidence-based medicine being better. My logical son nods and goes back to his video game.

When he was five, he asked why people believed in coincidences. Things, he reasoned, just happen. Why do people say they are connected?

He also thinks Santa Claus is stupid. Always has.

When the doctor comes in, my son puts away his phone. She's a resident with a silky ponytail. She asks more questions. Looks at the ankle. It's twice the size of the other one. He needs an X-ray. Then she turns to me.

"Any auto-immune diseases in the family?"

"Yes, I have ulcerative colitis."

I see her mentally flip through a list of possible diseases and know my history has entered the room. I keep my voice steady, hoping my son will hear only routine answers to routine questions. Nothing to worry about here.

The resident mumbles about how it could be other things, but he's too old for many of them, before settling on, "Let's get the X-ray and go from there."

Yes. Let's.

She asks if we know where radiology is and tries to explain. She doesn't usually work at this clinic. I say thanks, we'll find it and be back. It's almost five o'clock.

On the short walk over, we pass through a glass hall. I can see across the river. The skyline looks like it's been wrapped in wool. A friend's house is in the "be ready to evacuate" zone. That's only thirty-five minutes from here.

I mention the resident's bedside manner. I don't want to ask him directly, but I'm trying to figure out if my son is worried about anything she said. "This is likely just an injury. It would have been better to get the X-ray before speculating. She's new. She'll learn."

I'm annoyed at the resident for making me worry if my kid might be worried.

My son doesn't seem worried. He's hoping the café is open. He's hungry.

My stomach hurts.

I've always carried worry in my gut. Growing up Catholic, I took the "do not lie" commandment so to heart that I threw up when I lied. This stopped as I got older, but I still avoided lying because of the nausea it brought on.

Then, at thirty-six, I went for a colonoscopy and left with an auto-immune disease. Ulcerative colitis, cousin to Crohn's. In 1932, gastroenterologist Burrill Bernard Crohn and his colleagues identified a group of patients with inflamed small intestines. I like to imagine his peers giving Crohn the honor. "Burrill, your work on this disease that makes people shit themselves to death is so important. It should really be named after you."

My son comes out of the X-ray room and says he bets the technician is good with kids.

"What do you mean?" I ask, eyeing the technician with his straggly rat tail.

"He kept repeating my name. Kids like that. I don't know, he was just mellow."

"Maybe he was high," I say.

My son barely laughs.

We go back to the white and green room.

The animals on the wall are black silhouettes, and as we wait, I begin to imagine they are fleeing. Fire, rising water, higher temps. Statistically speaking, they should be worried. We all should be. My kids' science classes seem to be equal parts "isn't nature wonderful," and "if you're paying attention, you know we're fucked."

Like all parents, I want my son to feel safe so he can go out in the world and not always assume the worst. I want him to know most people asking for directions won't hurt you, although you need to keep an eye out. Most runny noses and coughs will get better on their own, but sometimes you need antibiotics. Most scientists agree that we're past a tipping point, and as a species, we're ….

Statistics tell me my son's swollen ankle is a sprain, a fracture at worse. I'm going to tell myself that story while we wait. I look at my healthy son playing a game on his phone. He's laughing, thrilled at his own performance, oblivious to the animals fleeing up the wall.

The resident with the ponytail comes back and pulls up the X-ray.

"The good news is, it's not a fracture." Then she catches herself. "I mean, there's no bad news. Come look."

We're looking at the inside of my son's body in black and white. She is pointing to an inch-long oval mass on the outside of the ankle bone. "This is causing the inflammation."

Ok, we've seen the evidence. So what is it?

She begins by saying, "benign cyst." Good start. Referral to orthopedics. They'll call tomorrow. All good. Then she keeps talking. Why is she still talking? We have an X-ray that suggests a benign cyst. We know nothing more. How about we wait until we have more evidence?

But she keeps talking.

"When you look at the report, it's going to say cancer, metastasis, things like that. But this is probably just a benign cyst."

She said cancer. Does she know she said cancer? And probably?

"So you think it's benign," I say. "You can tell that from the X-ray? Or do you need to do a biopsy?"

"Orthopedics will need to look at it. Sometimes these just go away on their own."

She said it could go away on its own. Cancer doesn't go away on its own. So she thinks it's a benign cyst. But she also didn't know what building we were in, and she just said we won't know until orthopedics reviews it.

I'm looking at my son, who is giving a thumbs-up to the resident. His way of saying, I'm hungry, we've been here for hours, can we go now.

I ask again, and she repeats, "orthopedics."

We're walking toward the car when it hits me. Did my son hear her say *cancer*?

He was ten when I was diagnosed. He remembers the surgeries, my bald head, the months of having to be quiet so I could sleep.

I drive home through the haze. My son switches through the radio. La-Z-Boy giveaway. Jesus loves you. He settles on "Margaritaville." The song came out in 1977, the year I was born.

I wonder if my friend's home is on fire.

I pick up my partner and our other son, who is twelve. Everyone is annoyed. We get the kids home, and I say, "Dad and I have to go get food." I call and order Tom Yum soup.

In the car, it's just the two of us. Me and my partner. The man who shaved my head, emptied my mastectomy tubes, made me laugh during chemo.

"What'd the doctor say?"

I'm driving down our street. "He has some kind of cyst or tumor and it's in an unusual place. She's going to call orthopedics tomorrow." I grip the wheel. "She showed us the X-ray. It looked big, on the outside of his ankle. Then she started talking about how we'll see words like cancer and metastasis on the X-ray report."

"What does that mean?"

"I asked if she could tell if it was benign from the X-ray or if we needed a biopsy. She said she'd have to talk to orthopedics. I know she's only a resident, but what the fuck!"

I can hear him breathing.

"She didn't say 'it's likely a benign cyst. We see them all the time in boys his age.' She didn't say that. Why didn't she say that? If she was really worried, she would have said … but she didn't … she …."

I pull into the parking lot. I rest my head on the cold steering wheel, and my partner stares out the front window.

We know exactly what happened in that waiting room with the little animals fleeing for their lives. I was triggered. Then I came home and triggered him.

That's what trauma does.

My history will invade my child's body. It already has in ways I cannot choose. But I don't want him to worry. So I tell him it's not a big deal, as my body screams because it remembers the MRI that turned into a big deal. The stomachache that led to an autoimmune disease. The pulled muscle that was a cancerous tumor.

The next day, an MRI is ordered. I keep telling myself the most likely scenario is it's a benign cyst. Yet any comfort I might take from "most likely" runs smack into my history, and my body says, fuck you.

My history. My body. A body that I want to believe ends at the tips of my fingers and the edges of my skin. A body I have learned to live in, believing that whatever they find, I can handle, because it is *my* body. *My* bones inside *my* skin. *Mine.*

But when that resident turned from my son's ankle and asked, "any history …," *mine* became *his*, and the walls of my body disintegrated. My son is my body is my history is my … teenager, who is hungry and needs a ride to school.

I know I'm privileged. I know things could be worse. When I talk about having cancer or ulcerative colitis, I always follow it up with, "I have good health insurance and a supportive family."

And yet, when my son's MRI comes back, and the tumor (no longer a cyst) is "likely benign" and requires an appointment with the orthopedic oncologist, my body isn't interested in how lucky we are. "Me" is now "him," and it is much harder to minimize *his* pain with a list of our privileges.

In *Intimations*, Zadie Smith tries to make sense of her own privilege during Covid. "By comparing your relative privilege with that of others," she writes, "you may be able to modify both your world and the worlds outside of your world—if the will is there to do it. Suffering is not like that. Suffering is not relative; it is absolute. Suffering has an absolute relation to the suffering individual—it cannot be easily mediated by a third term like 'privilege.'"

Suffering and its aftermath, trauma, don't reside in the realm of reason. They live in our muscles and cells. They grab us by our guts and piss on our arguments about privilege. And some days, they turn stupid wall decals of mice into rats, gnawing at your child's ankle.

Smith looked to the Stoics for practical assistance about how to live through a crisis. I never held my infant son and imagined he was dead, but after sitting in an exam room with my teenager and my history, I think the Stoics may have been onto something.

I heat up some soup and watch my son as he hunches at the kitchen table over a gigantic pumpkin. Like me, he's always loved to draw and make things. His gingerbread houses have ranged from pagodas to mid-century modern, and his *Aliens* Halloween costume would make Sigourney Weaver proud.

Using a Swiss Army knife, he flicks bits of orange from his finger, then stretches his spine over the chair back, pleased with himself. I walk over to admire his work. In beautiful medieval script, with flourishes worthy of an illuminated manuscript, he has carved, "Fuck Off."

"Lovely," I say. And I mean it. I see my child. I feel his delight. And in this moment, I am content with our history.

T.K. Schuberth holds an MFA from UC Riverside-Palm Desert and a Ph.D. in Philosophy of Religion from the University of Chicago, where they focused on gender, sexuality, and religion. They have had careers in finance and academics and were a Tin House 2020 workshop recipient. Their writing has appeared in *The Coachella Review*, *Litbreak Magazine*, and *The Copperfield Review*, and their unpublished novel, *Opening the Bodies*, was chosen as a Launch Pad 2022 Prose Top 50 manuscript.

ABECEDARIAN FOR AN INHERITANCE

Poetry by Andréa Ferrell Gannon

April, boxing Mother's estate:

bundles of crayon drawings, baby books, and Hallmark

cards. Congratulations! a baby girl. You're

disappointed—but she'll be Daddy's

every happiness. Date ordered,

filed docs: our relation's gangster days in evidence,

gay-bashing, road raging, steroid

hazes. For Dad: parole forms, prison

intakes: Rolaids, belt, watch, wallet. How they

joked that my place and Mom's were barefoot in the

kitchen, and I shot back how theirs was the inside of trouble. Next,

letters via aerogramme, agenda books embossed:

Mrs. RG Ferrell. Years full and glib. Jan. 1st resolutions so

neat: *always the same: don't leave the dishes till morning!*

Oh then a younger waitress and *RG gone early, then ball games all day, Andréa on*

   his chest.

Perhaps Dad was resting. For what was to come.

Quiet calendar squares. No more

Remembrances and don't-forgets, or birthdays like in '67 through '71:

  Pool with Toni and the kids. New BBQ. Mum and Dad for

Father's Day. A drive along the coast. Westwood art show.

Silence. I flipped through the hollowed months and heard

terrible weeks of watery pleas, *don't leave*

us. Grandad's writing, *those bloody Yanks. Their word is shite.*

      Scribbled info for that fall's flight to St. Albans. Mom just

Valerie again. She kept a photo of my

wedding dress, my sonograms—congratulations me! Not a double

X chromosome for miles. Excavating

yanks me back. I side-eye Mom's engagement ring and hear our echoes.

Zirconia and my condolences.

AS IF I KNEW WHAT I WAS DOING

Poetry by Andréa Ferrell Gannon

I caught four metros to get to your white sand,
  planted my ass, waited patient as moonlight,

faced the sea, an ear cocked to catch the glassy
  splinter of your approach. You asked, *Why'd you come?*

I asked, *Why'd you, motherfucker?* Words nudged us
  to the center of a Venn diagram, ten

    shy fingers rake fine Zen circles in the grain.

One day, we'd look back and laugh, but then it was like
  sitting in the front of class still, millions of eyes

pricking our skin, scalping us and burning. You
  lit a blunt. The smoke snaked to heaven and vine,

a shared halo. I carefully aligned my
  lips to the press and form of yours. I showed up for you and

    I could show you things like how I knew to blow

smoke from my nostrils—cool glide on the outside—
  to make you laugh and reach for me. More. I knew

things, baby, like how moonlight was my gloss and
  shadow; my high hope it turned cotton sequin,

split ends to beads; I hoped you'd hear their music
  calling through falling moon haze and

    you'd answer.

I think to call sometimes to explain

Poetry by Andréa Ferrell Gannon

to repaint the swimming pool and sky for you,

    Hockney blue and shadowless behind my dad's apartment.

Remember phoning nightly? *Meet me,* code for *walk half the road for me.*

    Those horrid June bugs, big as beach balls,

pinwheeling between lamplight and starlight.

    We clung to each other but delighted in being

barefoot and together, for sleepovers and tequila

    and yellow cloudless afternoon stretches—

you, frolicking and my trying, too.

    The pool walls abraded my stomach's tender skin

and knees when I hauled myself out to hunch

    reverse butterfly in a beach map towel, Mom's *Looking for Mr. Goodbar*

open on my thighs, yellowed pages pocked with water drops and chlorine.

    I thought to dry them with the red end of my cigarette.

I thought, if I were to rise and walk you would see me crumble

    while, your chin atop your forearms along the round concrete lip, you

chided my maturity, my sighs, cavernous as prehistory. I studied

    how my goggles and your soaked blondness made a garland

upon your brow. The landlord I didn't let you see,

    his shady silhouette, red eyes at the sliders. I spoke to you

only of the wrinkled, raucous MILF who

    stole my HS ring from the metal table

where I placed it for safekeeping

    its stone as blue and plastic as pool water and sky.

Andréa Ferrell Gannon, MFA, is a native Californian and the daughter of an English immigrant and a Lakota. She taught French and Spanish for many years, then English to adolescent refugees and immigrants. Find her now or soon in *The Washington Post, The Coachella Review, GRXL, Kelp Journal, Cricket,* and *Poet Lore.*

DEVIL CUT

Fiction by Robert Morgan Fisher

Blaine's father suggested they get a haircut together.

Blaine couldn't believe it when they pulled up to a civilian shop. A haircut was something they usually did on base and cost about five bucks. This was a men's *salon*, where hair was *styled*. All the rage in 1975, getting your hair styled. Blaine would've never expected his squared-away Air Force dad to go in for such an indulgence.

Nevertheless, there they were, in the dim, tacky, rococo red velvet sanctum of tonsorial decadence known as Le Man's on the outskirts of Dover, Delaware. Blaine had been allowed to move away from the military buzzcuts of his youth. Base barbers did their best to accommodate the longer hair trend by offering exotic-sounding things like razor cuts and not laughing when Blaine asked to have his hair feathered back. Even his father, Lieutenant Colonel Abner Wilhite, now actually allowed his own hair to touch his ears.

Still, Blaine was shocked at the suggestion they get their hair *styled*. Shocked and pleased. The senior Wilhite had been referred to Le Man's by a younger officer who said that Roy Deveaux was a pretty good barber and that it was really more like getting a haircut at your favorite watering hole. That Le Man's featured a full, open bar for customers was all the Lieutenant Colonel needed to hear.

Roy Deveaux ran Le Man's with Artie O'Shea, a hunched-over homunculus with white hair. Above Artie's possum nose, a pair of pince-nez glasses—below, Kurt Vonnegut-style mustache. The two chain-smoked while they worked and moved with the glacial slowness of the terminally hungover. They probably should've posted a liquor license, but the fact that drinks were complimentary and only for adult customers seemed to constitute a legitimate loophole. No one complained. Blaine and his father walked in to find two boozehound barbers, still recovering from the night before, listening to an endless 8-track loop of *The Mills Brothers Greatest Hits*.

Roy was slim, swarthy with a bouffant brushed-back helmet of thick brown hair and mutton-chop sideburns. Bushy black eyebrows arched over squinting, tobacco-brown eyes. His sharp, straight nose gave him the look of a Volaré—as Blaine's older sister Becky liked to describe Italian-American wise-guys who came off like Dean Martin singing that song. He wore short-sleeved shirts when he worked, so the heat was always turned up high in winter. On his right forearm, underneath the hair, a blurry tattoo of a bird with something in its talons, indecipherable writing above. He was classically handsome and cool in a retrograde way. Blaine assumed Roy had done time in prison.

The styling began with a shampoo. Blaine had never had another person (besides his mother when he was very young) shampoo his hair. He shut his eyes out of nervousness. When he lifted his right eyelid he saw an upside-down image of Roy smiling through a Benson & Hedges haze. Roy squinted while he massaged Blaine's scalp. After a rinse and towel-off, the chair was cranked upright, swiveled and the actual cutting began.

I'd like it feathered back, said Blaine.

That was the latest look, feathered back and parted in the middle. Roy nodded, took a deep drag, rested the cigarette in a full ashtray, exhaling through his nose. Blaine's father sat in a chair across the room, chatting volubly and sipping a martini while Artie O'Shea slowly nodded and trimmed.

What grade you in? mumbled Roy.

Ninth.

My daughter's in ninth.

What's her name?

Sailor.

Sailor Deveaux? I've heard about her! said Blaine.

In the mirror he saw Roy's lips flatten into a straight line. Blaine was vaguely aware he had misspoken, that not only did his words come out all wrong, but they were not at all what he meant to say. Yet, he inexplicably dug the hole a little deeper with:

Everyone knows Sailor. And finally, the nosedive coup de grace: She gets around.

Blaine shifted awkwardly in his chair. Roy didn't say anything, just kept cutting—albeit with a little more intensity than before. In the mirror, Dad wore a wounded look of embarrassed disbelief. Blaine averted his eyes.

On the drive home, Lt. Colonel Wilhite chewed his son out but good.

You *never* tell a man his daughter *gets around* for chrissake! He might've just heard this morning that she was knocked up or something.

Sorry, sir.

Blaine felt terrible. It was unlikely Sailor Deveaux was knocked up. She didn't have a loose or wild reputation. She was very pretty and popular. What Blaine was trying to say (and failed spectacularly) was that Sailor Deveaux was totally out of his league. Blaine was completely infatuated with Sailor. *Everyone* was in love with Sailor Deveaux—that's all Blaine was trying to communicate. The compliment, that he was among her legion of admirers, had caused him to bungle what were supposed to be earnest, benign words of praise.

Adding insult to injury: the haircut Roy gave Blaine was *horrific*.

Blaine looked like he was wearing a cabbage on his head.

His sister Becky laughingly described Blaine's haircut: Albino Liza Minnelli—after sticking her head in a blender.

Serves you right, said his father. Serves you right.

At school, Blaine's new haircut elicited howls of laughter in class, in the halls and at basketball practice.

He saw Sailor Deveaux in civics, but she looked right through him as usual. Sailor had Roy's dark eyes, mulatto skin. Just the slightest hint of dusky peach fuzz extending down from where she looped long straight hair back over her ears—which she did with her thumbs every few minutes, a nervous habit. On a boy, that fuzz would be fully-developed sideburns; on Sailor it seductively hinted at the dark, soft prize nestled between her legs. Several times Sailor caught Blaine looking at her. She'd frown as he quickly pretended to look past, cheeks combusting into burning blush.

After a few weeks, people grew bored with making fun of Blaine's hatchet job haircut. They gradually accepted it as a natural part of the freshman landscape, like a deformed tree.

Two months later Blaine's father suggested they go back to Le Man's for another styling. He wanted to get it right. But Blaine's hair was once again hacked to pieces by Roy, who was so hungover his hands were shaking.

Blaine's father put down his martini glass and suppressed a belch as he got up from his chair.

Say Roy—isn't it a little … uneven?

He looked to Artie O'Shea for some kind of backup, but Artie was opening and slamming drawers, searching for a fresh pack of Kents.

Latest style, muttered Roy, squinting through the haze of a fresh cig'. Delaware Devil Cut.

This passed for an acceptable explanation.

On Monday, the renewed jeers of Blaine's classmates.

Blaine learned a few things about his adversary: Roy was divorced, for one thing. Sailor's mom was no longer in the picture. This was unusual, as the mother usually got custody. There was no telling what innate wildness in Roy's ex-wife might have rendered her unfit for motherhood.

Whatever it was, Blaine knew that wildness was no doubt genetically encoded into Sailor. He could feel it, intuit it, just by looking at her. He fantasized about Sailor, gripping himself in the night. And when it came time for another haircut, he'd go back to Le Man's just to have his scalp massaged by the very hands that had helped preserve the imagined wantonness of Sailor Deveaux's unseen mother.

Every couple of months, like clockwork, the horrible haircuts continued.

Blaine actually had very nice hair—his mother's: thick, raven-black, wire-straight, malleable. But you'd never know that from his freshman and sophomore yearbook photos. His parents pleaded with him to stop going to Le Man's. The Lieutenant Colonel suggested, even ordered, that he try other places. But Blaine couldn't be persuaded. Though he'd long passed the point of paying penance for his previous conversational gaffe, he kept going back.

In a way Blaine hoped, absurdly, Sailor Deveaux might one day pass him in the hallway and really *see* him. *Your father made you and he made me.* Blaine prayed Sailor might recognize her own flower in the imperfect, lopsided—sometimes jagged—spray of hair crowning Blaine's head.

But she never did. Instead, the wildness germinating beneath the surface sprouted and blossomed into wicked rebellion.

Sailor began to let herself go, started smoking before and after school. Her breasts seemed to inflate overnight. Waist contracted, legs lengthened. Round cheeks disappeared, giving sharp definition to the woman within.

Older boys came calling. One of them a nineteen-year-old Army corporal who impregnated Sailor.

Details got murky; something about a shotgun wedding to avoid court martial and statutory rape charges. These were all second and third-hand stories—he didn't dare ask Roy about it.

That was Blaine's sophomore year. Next run-in with Roy resulted in a particularly bad mop-chop, so Blaine finally threw in the towel and stopped going to Le Man's.

Within a year, Artie O'Shea keeled over of a heart attack in mid-snip. There was an obit in the paper. Blaine started going to Supercuts and whenever he thought of Sailor Deveaux, he'd also think about Roy and how lonely he must be down at Le Man's all by himself.

Two years later, as Blaine was about to graduate, he came back to Le Man's with a special request:

Shave it off. I joined the Marines.

Roy lit a fresh Benson & Hedges off the old.

You don't wanna do that, he said.

What—join the jarheads?

No, the haircut. Don't do that.

Why not? said Blaine. Thought I'd give you a task equal to your level of skill.

Blaine had grown defiant and cocky. It was either the Corps or become a punk rocker. He'd cultivated a truckload of anger and attitude. Roy Deveaux's shitty haircuts were only a footnote on Blaine's extended inventory of personal and societal grievances. Roy squinted and shook his head.

Ain't gonna do it.

Why the hell not?

You're gonna want *them* to cut it.

What do *you* know about it?

Was a Marine once.

No way.

I was.

Roy leaned against the shampoo sink, displayed his tattoo which Blaine now realized said Semper Fi. Roy was still thin as a whippet—no more than a twenty-six-inch waist. Blaine, however, had been working out for over a year, biceps like canned hams.

You were a jarhead?

Yeah, Korea.

Don't look old enough.

I was young once, said Roy. Anyway, when you show up and they shear your head, it's like a rite of passage. It's important. If you show up bald, you'll be sorry.

Blaine said, All right.

He started to leave.

Roy pushed him back down.

I'll cut your hair. You'll want to look presentable.

Blaine gave it some thought, then agreed.

Roy did the usual: shampoo and cut, didn't say a word the whole time. He worked the lather in, almost tenderly. It was weird. Blaine was tempted to ask candid questions about Sailor, to maybe provoke Roy. Blaine had heard Roy's daughter was now divorced. He wanted to know if Sailor was planning on returning to Dover to graduate. But now that Roy had talked him out of shaving his head, Blaine wasn't sure what to say or do. He was just about to ask about Sailor when Roy spun him around to face the mirror and murmured, Voila.

This time Roy had given Blaine a real styling. It was the ultimate cut, feathered back and everything. Blaine looked like a brunette Robert Redford.

Wow, he said.

On the house.

It'll be gone in two weeks.

Well then, enjoy it, said Roy. Put it to good use.

Whatever that meant. Roy wouldn't even take a tip.

He shook Blaine's hand and said, *Death Before Dishonor.*

Blaine was glad he didn't step off the bus at Parris Island with a cue ball head. Roy was right about that. Recruits who showed up with their heads already shaved were treated differently—and not in a good way.

And, four years later, when Roy headed out to the base to welcome Blaine's body back from Beirut, Sailor asked him where the hell he thought he was going. Roy said he was stepping out to get some cigarettes. Sailor started up a shrill harangue about how she had a date, and who's gonna watch the kids, et cetera.

Roy told his daughter that what she didn't know could fill a book.

Robert Morgan Fisher won the 2021 Montana Humor Prize, the 2018 Chester Himes Fiction Prize, was shortlisted for the 2019 John Steinbeck Award and was runner-up for the 2021 *Saturday Evening Post* Great American Fiction Prize. His fiction and essays have appeared in numerous anthologies and literary journals including *The Saturday Evening Post, Upstreet, Pleiades, The Arkansas Review, Red Wheelbarrow, The Missouri Review Soundbooth Podcast, The Seattle Review, The Spry Literary Journal, 34th Parallel, The Journal of Microliterature, Spindrift, The Rumpus,* and many other publications. He teaches creative writing at UCLA and Antioch University. (www.robertmorganfisher.com)

NINETY MILES FROM NORMAL

Nonfiction by Christina Dillow

Forty-five minutes had passed when the compact helicopter crossed over the county line intersecting the Las Padres National Forest with the sea. Vaguely aware of my circumstances, I lay swaddled in a thick medic bag, unable to move. Beeping gauges and gurgling IV bags dangled above me in a symphony of lifesaving sounds in harmony with the vibrational hum of the floorboards. But my brain had been chemically tuned to a different channel, where timeless melodies soothed the soul. A sudden drop in altitude overtook the pharmaceutical bliss as erratic sundowner winds bullied us into a bumpy descent—shaken not stirred. The copilot hung in the open door of the hovering craft, leaping as his foot touched the rooftop pad, swinging open my side door and revealing an expansive Santa Barbara sunset adorned with a skyline of fan palm trees waving in the wind. A team of masked nurses rushed towards us as I was rolled onto a stretcher and fitted with clear plastic muzzle. On countless occasions over the last year, I had joked that my next vacation was going to be in the hospital. Apparently, the universe had been listening. Breathe ... three, two, one .... A creamy pastel palette of reds and yellows faded into gray.

It was dark when I awoke to hushed female voices and the soft clinks of metal jangling like keys on a ring. Fuzzy memories of my air ambulance episode surfaced, and with considerable effort over the next hour, I came to understand I was in post-op, where a critical care nurse was training another nurse how to prepare the external ventricular drain which had been threaded through a hole drilled in my skull only a few hours before. Together the nurses braided, unbraided, and cinched lines together matching "A" to "A" and "B to B" and so forth. Later I would learn that the squeaky contraption next to me was a body-length level with elementary school sized numbers so that my nurses could measure the precise incline of my body and head, ensuring that gravity could assist in removing the blood from my brain. My eyes had adjusted to dim digital light radiating from the monitors. To my left, I could see a counter with a few drawers and cabinets. On my right, a recliner chair. Then, the room unceremoniously filled with painfully bright light as one of the nurses pulled open the heavy drape covering a sliding glass window and door. I had a front-row seat where a lone nurse sat yawning at the helm of a long U-shaped counter. The large clock mounted above my door ticked 3:30 a.m.

Four hours later, I opened my eyes to a workplace bustling with activity in total contrast to Hopper's *Nighthawks* scene I had witnessed earlier. I lifted my heavy body and swung my legs over the side of the bed, sending a screeching alert to my new nurse, who was writing her name on the dry erase board. Ashley was quick on her feet to reach me, ordering me to stay in bed. Rest was the short list for the day. I was hungry and told her so. "We'll get to that," she assured me.

I studied her hazel eyes above her surgical mask as she listened to my lungs. Soon a steaming bowl of oatmeal arrived, accompanied by a plastic mug of black coffee. There were no dietary restrictions in place, so for lunch I ordered a spinach salad with blue cheese crumbles, bacon, pecans, and raspberry vinaigrette. Hospital food California style. An hour after breakfast, a trio of doctors peered at me from outside the glass, flipping through pages on my chart, apparently evaluating my condition. It seemed strange that they did not enter the room or ask me any questions. But *strange* in the days of the pandemic had become the order of the day. A male nurse who had stopped to confer with the doctors now stepped up to my bedside.

"So how much alcohol do you drink? I mean, how many drinks per day? Do you have a history of alcoholism? Who's your primary care doctor? Have you had a stroke before?"

As I lingered in a state of fragile mortality, my heart knew it was time to rewrite the story and face his query head-on. But my ego liked the old story and was holding court, skirting the issue.

"Well," I said, "I'm a chef. I own a restaurant. I'm from a restaurant family. We drink."

Apparently, my body was not only dealing with the aftermath of a life-threatening subarachnoid brain hemorrhage, but it was also doing so in the throes of alcohol withdrawals and all the subsequent biochemical challenges. Something called *salt-wasting* and whatever difficulty it was causing inside my body was a huge concern, as was something known as *vasospaslm*, which could cause a fatal stroke at any time during the initial healing process. I had beat the odds the day before, but I still hovered in the limbo of a critical time period. Despite playing dodgeball with death, I continued to defend my daily drinking habit. The fact was I had spent the better part of my fifty-something years learning about and loving wine, as far back as celebrating my sweet sixteenth birthday party in a private room of an iconic dinner house toasting my family with a glass of Perrier-Jouet. I had been hooked! Wine was an integral part of my restaurant career. We lived in the once unknown wine region called Paso Robles, now world-renowned. I could easily name many appellations within our county, a number which had grown exponentially during my forty-year span in the hospitality industry, making it challenging for me to balance restaurant demands and moderate drinking habits. My thirty-six-year marriage to a career bartender added to the equation. This story is different though; it's not about a lifelong battle with alcohol abuse (though it could be), it's a story of universal elements coalescing in a *come to Jesus* moment of change.

It had only been a month since the entire world was turned upside-down in a state of panic caused by a coronavirus, or as the Gen-Xers had dubbed it across Instagram, "The Rona." As unbelievable as it was, strict *social distancing* mandates had been ordered. Suddenly, every public place had premeasured cautionary stickers on the floor indicating where to stand to follow the new *six feet* edict. It seemed that everyone was suspicious of one another. There was the possibility one could be infectious, and it still wasn't clear how the virus spread. Surgical masks in all styles and colors became a fashion statement, with debates holding forth over whether they helped or hindered. Our governor had ordered everyone to isolate at home, which meant the full closure of all nonessential businesses—my restaurant included. Not liquor stores though. *So even the government agreed that imbibing was acceptable.* My well-being was usually balanced by inspirational reading and introspective practices, however, when the lockdowns were enforced, a volcano of anger and resentment erupted from deep within me. I held stubbornly to my convictions, which added to my anxiety. I considered myself a peacekeeper. I needed balance which I found by putting my thumb on the scale. Relief was readily at hand with a bottle of wine opened early in the day. Many people I knew in the hospitality industry were finding ways to turn a devastating situation into an opportunity for increased family time or were busy homeschooling, working-out with weights, walking, or learning how to make sourdough bread. Not me. I spent my days isolated in my empty restaurant, worrying about how to surf the wave of online ordering and curbside delivery. It was certainly no way to make a living without full production, but I had laid off my entire staff. I remember reposting a clever meme circulating on Facebook: *When the pandemic ends which will you be? A hunk, a drunk, a monk, or a chunk.* Monk resonated but drunk galloped into the lead. *I'm from a restaurant family. We drink.* And though people around me were settling into this new sense of time and space, I was in a downward spiral amplified by terrifying scenes of human suffering and relentless ticker tape death toll counts blaring on the television. I decided to unplug it, though heaving it through a window crossed my mind. Newscasters were the new experts on everything. Civilization was in peril.

We roared up Highway One, passing a picturesque stretch of shoreline flanked by a desolate pier on one side and a famous castle a thousand feet up on the other. A few miles further, the rocky coastline yielded to a restless sea, a crescendo of waves crashing mere yards from our car, a gold Cadillac El Dorado. For my stepdad, Ron, bigger was always better. I lowered the window, enjoying the salty brume on my face. The last fugitive beams of sunlight broke through, spotlighting a single fishing boat chugging north a hundred yards or more from the beach. Serenaded by a raucous band of seagulls, the bow of the boat dunked and dipped like an out-of-step dance partner.

I envisioned a small crew huddled on deck, hands cupped over lit cigarettes, poles secured, slack lines wound tight—a strenuous day behind them. Where were they going? Did they sleep on the boat overnight? How could they possibly sleep in such turbulence? My mind was filled with so many unanswered questions.

For the last year, I'd been navigating through my own turbulent adolescence, in search of an elusive freedom hampered by the duality of a divorced family, complicated by an upwardly mobile stepdad who seemed to have no empathy for kids. Ron never considered the trauma induced by frequently moving to yet another new address, each house improved on the outside, but emptier on the inside—a fitting metaphor of our life.

During middle school, our newest house in the valley had an elegant blue and green marble entry with a gaudy crystal chandelier hanging in the center, leading to an empty formal living room on the left and a comfortable family room just beyond. We couldn't afford to furnish the living room, so I claimed it as my personal theater, setting up a cheap turntable in the corner, albums fanned out on the floor around it. Queen's *Bohemian Rhapsody* was not endowed with the popular disco dance beat I so loved, but it had a unique style with poetic lyrics that felt good to sing. And sing I did, a passion inspired by my paternal grandparents who played piano and sang operetta professionally for years. Renowned in our hometown of Whittier, they were hired to sing a duet at a fundraiser for Nixon as he climbed the political ladder. Moving from town to town eventually took us further from our grandparents and the emotional support we had counted on since our dad had remarried and moved to Seattle. Music was the thread binding me. Hopefully, this short road trip would help settle my confusion. The end of a challenging year, concluding with a new habit of smoking Virginia Slims, easily acquired at gas station vending machines for fifty cents a pack.

Familiar ocean smells tugged at my memory, taking me back another half a dozen years before my mom began accepting invitations to martini hour at our neighbor's house. Before the yelling began. We had been a happy family boating to Catalina Island with our dad, George, whose smile was wide and welcoming. He was confident and carefree at the helm of a twenty-six-foot sailboat he had masterfully built by hand in his family's yard. It was during that arduous two-year project, while he was still in high school, that he had met our mother-to-be, Joan, at a beach party in Alamitos Bay. They belonged to rival high schools three miles apart, making it convenient to date over the next year. They eventually eloped to Vegas, curtailing my dad's dream of sailing the world. Soon, a baby was on the way. Three more would follow in nearly as many years. My dad was a dreamer, an artist, and a craftsman who did not belong in an office job, though he kept trying. He longed for sun and the sea. My mom was raising four kids and coming of age in the women's movement when she took a job as a hostess in a swanky steakhouse where Ron was the kitchen manager. He must have had whatever it was she longed for.

Ron piloted his gold El Dorado like a speedboat, traversing craggy bluffs and blind curves with reckless abandon, causing my stomach to loop and tumble, finally finding equilibrium as the curves opened to a long straightaway bound for infinity. Ron never missed an opportunity to make up for lost time; he was gaining on the red dot ahead of us, quickly arriving at the tailgate of an old Ford truck. Infamously impatient, he craned his head to see around the rusty relic burdened with bales of hay. His foot pumped like a drum staccato back and forth from gas pedal to brake, finally landing heavily on the gas, launching us like a missile into the opposite lane. Uncharacteristically cool, my mother turned to check on her two teenagers in the spacious back seat. My brother, Don, two years my senior, was surprisingly silent. Hunkered down just high enough to read the speedometer over the straight line of the front seat—eighty miles per hour and climbing! My mom knew all too well that my stepdad loved living on the edge. He delighted in scaring people by doing crazy things on a whim—or a wager. Once, we had been driving through downtown Los Angeles on the way to Chinatown for dinner. We passed through an area known as Skid Row, where we had left my oldest brother, Steve, at the Greyhound bus terminal heading to Seattle to live with our dad. Ron was particularly giddy on that night, as he and Steve butted heads constantly. It was then he proclaimed he was tired of *all* us kids, and he abruptly turned into a commercial loading zone where he announced that Don and I should get out of the car. Since we *all* thought we were smarter than the grown-ups, he was sure we could find our own way home. His belly laugh was maniacal as he sputtered and coughed and assured my mom he was only joking. Eventually, I learned to see through my stepdad's follies, most of which were never that funny, though a few might have been normal as parental gags go. But on that day in December—traveling a nearly deserted coastal highway at harrowing speeds—this family was ninety miles from normal.

Christmas Eve in Big Sur was magical. We savored dinner before a magnificent circular fireplace in a restaurant built hundreds of feet above the sea. Afterwards, Don and I shared a slice of chocolate layer cake while my mom and Ron sipped hot toddies from the bar. Half an hour later, the four of us ambled down a steep concrete stairway illuminated by ambient lantern light. A wedge of parking lot barely big enough for the ten cars that filled it lay at the bottom. A few minutes' drive up the road, a rustic log cabin lodge sat camouflaged amidst the redwood forest flanked by a roaring river. Inside, Ron and my mom played rounds of backgammon in front of a toasty fire. They were arguing about her infamous loss a few weeks earlier, one we would all like to forget. As punishment for that loss, she elected to roll a martini olive around the neighborhood with her nose in lieu of eating a whole fiery habanero pepper out of the jar. Now, as Ron was recounting the moment, chiding her about being a sore loser, she abruptly flipped the board, sending brown and white pieces flying across the room. Thankfully, those losses were balanced with the occasional win. The most memorable resulted in ten-speed bikes for us all. Don and I sat outside and watched smoke dance around a campfire, enjoying the rich perfume of the ancient evergreens.

This was the first of many road trips to Big Sur in my lifetime, but none was more significant. On the way home, seventy miles south of Big Sur, Ron decided to veer off the highway into a touristy small town. He drove slowly along a main street marked "business route." It was unusual for Ron to slow down—he was always in hurry, but not that day. Having escaped the grueling ten-hour shifts he spent as regional manager for a restaurant group called Far West Services, he was now in the process of opening his third new upscale steakhouse. He had a knack for success in an industry filled with failure. But unbeknownst to us kids, there had been talk about escaping Los Angeles for good. Our older sister, Lyn, had moved into her own apartment off Reseda Boulevard and was heading to college that fall, while our older brother—"the mad scientist"—intended to join the Air Force to pay for his schooling; he had just passed his GED, aged sixteen.

Ron parallel parked in front of a big window, barely clearing the crosswalk. It was his lucky day as he read "Restaurant for Sale." Double jackpot: a bar next door. Without hesitation, like a dowsing wand bending towards water, he headed that way. The historic saloon was the town gathering place and bustled with characters, a melting pot of cultures—cowboy boots jingling with spurs, long flowing skirts in a myriad of bright colors, and greasy blue collars that hadn't seen a washing machine in weeks. A few out-of-place tourists were scattered amongst the crowd, and a thick vinyl banquette and glossy dark tables lined the south wall where a collection of empty cocktail glasses and beer bottles proliferated.

Camozzi's Saloon could have been a museum, walls and ceilings layered with items dating back a hundred years. Leather hats, marriage certificates, family photos, lassos, business licenses all enshrined in reminiscence of someone special or of times past. Patrons perched on barstools watching the bartender perform at the antique bar. Others ate popcorn while awaiting their turn at the slightly pitched snooker table in the back by the stage. Moe Bandy blared from the jukebox in the corner.

East Village was the older part of town, downtown to the locals, where you would find a liquor store, two small grocery stores, a post office, and a Bank of America which looked like it belonged on the set of *Gunsmoke*. Around the corner was 'Round the Corner Cafe, second only to the saloon for storytelling and conviviality.

Mom handed us each a ten-dollar bill as we left her at the saloon door. Ron was already steps ahead of her inside, where he hoped to get the scoop on the Italian place next door. We took note of the timeline we were given and decided to explore the two square blocks comprising the town business district, then headed towards an empty dirt lot hoping to find access to a creek that appeared to run behind the town. My brother stopped in front of a dilapidated building crowned with a faded sign: Ralph's T.V. & Gun Shop. Intrigued, we stepped in, a ribbon of bells announcing our entry, but there was no sign of life. Floor-to-ceiling metal shelves of all shapes and sizes lined dingy walls, and shorter shelves created a sort of maze through the middle of the large space. Looming above and crammed onto shelves were boxes of every age and size, some labeled Sony or Magnavox, others Panasonic and RCA. There were games like Monopoly and Clue in dusty piles lost alongside necessities like toasters and light bulbs. And there were guns. Thankfully locked in a glass case behind the counter. As we made our way towards the back of the store, a man wearing a rubber pig snout jumped out at us: "Boo!" He asked if he could help us find anything and chuckled as he introduced himself as the proprietor, Ralph. He was dressed neatly in a white short-sleeved, collared shirt tucked into tan polyester pants. His slicked-back charcoal hair formed a peak over his bushy gray eyebrows, which rustled as he removed the snout. Don thanked Ralph, and grabbed my arm. "We were just looking, he said, and we bolted out the back door, landing on a couple of milk crates discarded above the creek behind the grocery store. Catching our breath, we watched a sturdy farmer climb out of his truck, nodding a friendly smile our way. His gigantic hands easily lifted an overflowing metal barrel over his head, spilling rotten produce onto a tarp in the bed of his truck. He seemed happy to answer a few questions my brother asked as he tied the corners like a knapsack before driving away.

Back in the car, we resumed the three-hour drive back to the city. Don recounted meeting a farmer who had been collecting food scraps to feed his four-hundred-pound hogs. I was about to tell my mom about creepy Ralph when she spoke the biggest news of the day: over cocktails at Camozzi's, they had bought the restaurant. We moved four months later.

The working-class people of Cambria lived hospitality—and partying! The population sign along Highway One may have read fifteen hundred, but in the summer season that number multiplied as hundreds of second homes filled with families escaping the heat of the Central Valley and hordes of tourists descended upon Hearst San Simeon State Monument fifteen minutes north. We were fortunate to buy The Caffe Porta Via at the beginning of an economic recovery and subsequent building boom, affording my parents the purchase of our rented building and an extensive remodel which would double the restaurant space. Locals watched as an impressive transformation took place. In a two-year period, Ron and my mom had turned a casual pizza parlor with sawdust on the floor into a contemporary Italian dinner house accented with hand-thrown ceramic tableware and linens made by a local seamstress. But it was the warm hospitality and five-star food my mom was dishing up from her tiny kitchen that was making memories. Customers looked forward to stopping at the open Dutch door in front of the stove and toasting my mom, who could usually be found with a glass of champagne in her hand. Conspicuously missing was Ron, but those same customers knew where to find him—he had a well-worn path from the kitchen door through the alley to the bar next door. Every half hour or so, he'd pop back into the restaurant in between snooker games to chat with the regulars.

Six years into a successful restaurant venture, Ron's drinking and gambling habits had taken a toll on every aspect of their life together, and alcohol had never been my mom's friend, triggering rage and leaving her sick in bed the next day. She courageously decided to find freedom from the chaos and filed for divorce, taking sole ownership of the restaurant with the help of my sister and her husband. Together, they gave it a heroic effort, but they couldn't find a way to climb out of debilitating debt. She struggled emotionally as she shut down the restaurant, forfeiting the property to the landlord who held the note. I don't think my mom ever completely recovered from the losses and traumas she experienced in her early life, though as fate would have it, that misfortune led to a chance meeting with the man she would marry and share the rest of her life with.

By the time I was twenty, I had held eight different restaurant jobs, always seeking something more. Hospitality became my focus and connecting with people my gift. I found it natural to talk with customers and built a strong following, leading to a handful of lifelong friendships. At this same time in my life, I was an aspiring photographer, having pledged never to follow my mom's career path. I enjoyed learning about f-stops and apertures and loved the solitude of a darkroom, practicing

Ansel Adams' Zone System techniques from a textbook. Occasionally, friends called me to shoot a wedding or a senior portrait package, but I found myself sick with worry until the results of my efforts were in hand, which could take days in the era of film; there were never any guarantees how the photos would turn out once they were processed. The comfort of food and hospitality always won me back.

On my twenty-third birthday, I opened my first restaurant in the town of Harmony, a venture friends and family urged me not take. With my mom's recipes in hand, I had negotiated a good lease, and since I did not know how to cook, I began my search for a business partner. A week later, while working a host shift at a local restaurant, a friend handed me a note written on a cocktail napkin delivered from Camozzi's: "Am interested, call me. Buttercup." I had never met Kathy, which was surprising in a small town, but serendipity was at play, as she was a cook at a popular lunch spot looking to open her own place. She had a great following, adding to the potential for success. Many of my mom's customers were excited for a chance to enjoy her food again, and within two months the Harmony Pasta Factory was born: "Where good friends and fresh pasta make for tasteful conversation." On the weekends, it was standing room only. Our success led to years of festivities enjoyed by locals and tourists alike—a creative artist enclave fueled by food, music, art ... and lots of wine!

Over the years, my story continued to weave a pattern much like my mom's. At times, it was difficult to tell them apart, yet different in so many ways, like looking at fragments of a broken mirror, each a reflection of success and loss. It was during my three-week recovery in the hospital that I began to pick up those pieces. I took a selfie video in my hospital bed, reminding my future self to never forget the pain I was enduring physically and to remember the damage my daily drinking habit had caused in my life. I was facing some hard truths about my own destructive patterns and the choices I had made, most of which had been hashed out *ad nauseam* in the pages of my journals spanning forty years—a lifetime of seeking answers to a millennium of questions. But there is nothing like a near-death experience to give quick answers. Because of the pandemic, I had been isolated, with no visitors, a rare opportunity to spend time with myself, to go within, and to understand the answers, which had always been there. After ten days of suffering and sleepless nights, my inner voice was loud and could not be ignored: *Chris! Let go!* In an instant, I got it. It was time to surrender and face my story, to embrace it. And with childlike wonder, I handed it all over to a higher power— "God" or "Source" or "Universe" or "Soul"—all names with the same life-altering resonance. Sometimes I call it "Flow" because it reminds me to be more like a twig floating on a river. A river of time. A river of memories. *I'm from a restaurant family.*

Christina Dillow has enjoyed writing, photography, and culinary arts since her high school days in Cambria, California. She has exhibited her photographs locally over the years but is most passionate about running restaurants. Her most recent restaurant, Fig, closed in 2020 after an eleven-year run. She's been happily married to artist Dennis Dillow since 1984. They live in Atascadero, California.

WHEN I WAS FIVE

Poetry by Lewis Leicher

When I was five, I accidently learned how to ride
a bike without training wheels: those miniature rear tires
became loose enough to slide backward and lift up
from the sidewalk, no longer providing any training.
I wasn't an intrepid kid … risk-taking did not come
easily to me (still doesn't)—I'd put my faith
in those ingenious magic wheels to keep me safe.
They were removed that very day and thrown away.

At eight, a bigger bike gave me more independence:
trips into town with friends or to the public library.
In Fifth Grade, my bike and I delivered evening papers—
we had those then. At fourteen, I got a pale yellow ten-speed,
with hand brakes, and pretended to race. In my thirties,
I had a dark green bike with tough wide tires and many gears,
riding it in Central Park, along Chicago's Lake Shore Drive,
and on vacations and long weekends in the Berkshires,
where my then-spouse and I rented tandems sometimes.

I started wearing a helmet when we all did—no more
wind-in-my-hair no-hands downhills. Lately, I've used only
exercise bikes (to save my creaky knees)—maybe I'll try
some flat-ground rides or an e-bicycle with a small motor
to help me climb inclines. Still, in a trial-and-error life
of ever-better bikes, of pedaled spoke-and-wheel fantasies,
I will always remember the scaled-down no-frills one
that tricked me into growing up … at least a little.

DECEMBER 1972

Poetry by Lewis Leicher

We all have personal landmarks—public places that matter
to us for private reasons, with no brass plaques to say why.
My favorite was the big wooden phone booth, in the lobby
of a midtown New York hotel, where I first really kissed a girl
       I was in love with, in December '72.

We'd met the prior summer at a camp in Vermont. I can't
recall why, but she was visiting the City before Christmas.
For those in later generations: pay phones were everywhere then
and everyone used them. Calls cost ten cents. For my peers and elders:
       remember … indoor booths used to be cleaner.

I visited my landmark occasionally over the years until
the hotel, which opened in 1912, converted to apartments
in the mid-1980s. Progress, for some … but why
didn't my personal Landmarks Preservation Commission
       save that beautiful oak booth from demolition?

Instead, it exists solely in memory, mine and probably hers
and maybe some hotel guests'—we were, after all, a real-life
big-city-teen-romance-movie cliché (not that I knew that then).
But how can genuine passion ever be clichéd? That could
       have been engraved on the non-existent plaque.

I won't be using her name. I don't kiss and tell, not even
after decades. *But how can embraces from so long ago
feel like they happened just yesterday?* Our landmark is gone,
but my love for her kisses lives again, when I close my eyes
       and pretend that an old phone booth welcomes us in.

WHAT I MISS MOST

Poetry by Lewis Leicher

Why, when I close my eyes, do I still see a city?
Buildings piled high, bees flying from dumpster to dumpster,
yellow cabs blooming in the streets. Mid-July in Manhattan,
90° by 10:00 A.M.—the cracked sidewalks, trying to
perfect their tans, are getting sunburned. No air conditioning
at home, I go to an early movie, where it's freezing.

In 1980, as I entered my mid-twenties,
I had a job typing on a Wang Word Processor
weekday evenings (5:00 to 10:00). Personal computers
were not widely available yet. For a young writer,
access to a true editing machine was life-changing.

I worked on the forty-fifth floor of a building on Broadway,
with a view of Clinton (aka Hell's Kitchen), the piers,
the Hudson, and the New Jersey horizon. The sun setting
below the clouds and the pollution turned the twilight sky
into a portrait painted by Impressionist angels: posed
in a pewter and slate blue uniform, with four silver stars
and vivid ribbons of indigo, crimson, copper, and gold.

I'd bring café con leche from a Cuban-Chinese place
and work quietly, by myself. Usually, there was no one
else around for that shift, except the security guards.
It was so peaceful. Once, I saw a big dragonfly fly by
my window—or was that a drone from another world?

The weekends felt like they lasted much longer than
the allotted two or three days, and the seasons seemed
to change more frequently than quarterly. There were millions
of people to watch and I watched them, in their natural
habitats—eating and drinking, talking and walking
(or rollerblading)—and saw that some were watching me.
I'd fallen in love with the City—fascinated and charmed,

as so many are, by the variety, the history,
the pace, and that too-famous, it-never-sleeps,
bright-neon-dream-(and/or-nightmare) quality.

Like many twenty-somethings, I tried on personalities
and changed them pretty frequently. Some were so different
they tuned into different FM stations: a few loved rock,
punk, and new wave; two favored disco and its dance descendants;
one chose jazz and American standards; another classical.
I still like those, as well as folk, country, pop, blues, R&B
and reggae, and their over-hyphenated collaborations.

"Personalities" sounds too jargon-y—"personal styles"
is a more accurate, though stilted, description. I'd like
to think that each of those old personal styles remains a part
of me, but lots of things I did back then now make me cringe,
including most of the clothes I chose and the drugs I did.
Still, some of those lost "me"s were way more fearless than I can
ever hope to be again—those personalities I miss.

Lewis Leicher has returned to poetry, now that he has retired, after an
almost forty-year break (for which poetry has not yet forgiven him).
During that break, he worked as an attorney, including for almost
twenty years for WebMD. He has lived in San Diego since 2001 and,
before that, lived mostly in and around New York City.

THE LIGHT OF LUNA MADRE

Fiction by C.S. Perryess

The icy night wind strikes me in the face. It pushes my back against the adobe graveyard wall. Such a wind, born high in the Juarapa Mountains—born of snow and ice.

Along the way, through the high deserts of Buitre Blanca, such a wind collects ghosts and cactus needles. Perhaps Adolfo is right. Perhaps I am still a child—my ghosts and needles are child's play. Still, I would sooner dwell on such things than the task before me.

I force myself into the chill—into the moaning wind—toward the grave of Sister Lucia Maria, the shovel frozen in my hand, the hammer heavy on my belt.

I know they are watching. They sit in Adolfo's workshop. They smile and laugh and slap one another's backs. The ale and the companionship keep them warm, not to mention the woodfire I built, lit, and tended.

I push into the wind. My thin-soled shoes crunch the frosted sand, past the resting place of Old Señora Garcia, past little Aldo Marquez, and past the marble angel who flies forever in the place of Ana Teresa Campos.

It is a cruel thing they make me do, but I am the woodworker's apprentice—Adolfo's boy. What choice have I?

Mother Moon winks once through the clouds, then deserts me. I am alone with the village shovel, stumbling the last twenty paces. I lean into the wind, though it slashes at my face. Behind me, my serape flaps like boneless wings, and I am there.

Sister Lucia Maria, I am so sorry. My actions are not my own. You remember me? Compact, you said, hardworking, Adolfo's boy? You remember Adolfo? A fine woodworker, yes, but a man of superstition, a man of mean spirit.

It is not an easy thing to cross oneself among needles and ghosts, with a shovel frozen to one's hand. I look from one hand to the other. Each one seems a dull, frozen ache at the end of an arm. I watch as those hands place the shovel, as my poor frozen foot rises, then rests, then stomps down. The blade of the shovel slices into the frozen grit.

I dig and dig. The wind stops for a breath and from behind me—from the workshop—a laugh cuts through the night. The pale eye of Luna Madre—Mother Moon—flashes down from the clouds, perhaps for a better look. What does she think of this sorry little village, of this slashing wind, of the woodworker's apprentice digging at the grave of Sister Lucia Maria?

What does she think of Adolfo, who brags that he arrived here a young boy with little more than a hammer and his skill? That he will never leave—not even for supplies—not for a solitary thing? That they will name the place after him? What does she think of a poor village's most prosperous man, a man with more coins than kindness, a man who never had one thought for the good works of Sister Lucia Maria?

The gritty rhythm of the shovel brings me back, stopping with a dull thud sooner than one would expect. I suck in a frozen breath and look down, but all is in shadow. I reach in with the blade of the shovel to scrape free a small sector of the rough, pine box.

Poor Sister—even this indignity—no more than three hands below the surface. All goes dark. Luna Madre has pulled close her veil of clouds, too ashamed to know what I must do.

A distant flash of light skitters over the headstones and tired wooden crosses—someone has opened the workshop door. My shadow stretches softly over the grave, into the night. A yell, maybe a laugh, who knows? Of all things, the wind shows mercy, garbling the sound, throwing it back into the throat where it began. The blackness of my shadow suddenly expands to cover all. The workshop door has been shut.

It is an effort opening my hand enough to drop the shovel. I kneel on the frosty sand, but cannot see into the gloom. Still, I know what is there. Who would know the pine box of a Sister of Poverty better than Adolfo's boy? Who would know the precise dimensions, the random placement of the knots, the pitchy scent as the handsaw makes its perfect cut? Who would know Adolfo's orders to use the worst of the wood, to spend no valuable effort or time on the box of a crazy old woman?

Who would remember arriving here in the back of a coughing old truck on a rainy autumn night—a boy, too young to be on his own in an angry village suspicious of newcomers? Who might recall one friendly soul of six dozen inhabitants? Who might remember kind words, a shared wooden bowl of thin, strangely sweet soup, a rusty cot and a red wool blanket?

I reach my stiff hands into the grave, brushing sand across the box. Sister Lucia's hands were bent and knotted. My hands cannot feel the slivers I know are piercing them. It is certainly the least I can do.

The wind howls from the Juarapas, over the Buitre Blanco, over the graves, over this kneeling apprentice woodworker, to Adolfo's shop. I imagine their open-mouthed laughs, their off-key songs, but the wind somehow sucks the sound from the picture in my mind. They silently reel, pour more ale, slap one another's backs, laugh at the foolish apprentice sent out into the night.

My hands sweep in numb arcs across the box from sides to center. I scoop up the gritty mounds of sand. I drop the handfuls at my side to form a tiny pile.

Adolfo had left me to build the box. He would never come check my work. He had taught me well how to build a box, even of the saddest pine, how to compensate for warped wood, how to set the nails just so, how to deliver the box, not with his cart, but balanced on my back.

Adolfo would never inspect it, just as he had never taken a second look at Sister Lucia, at me. He would collect his pay for my work, a few coins from the other Sisters, then he and his compadres would disappear until the sun dropped and the cold set in.

After putting poor Sister in the ground, I waited, shivering in the workshop, the workspace brushed, the floor swept, the fire set for his return. As the winds howled and the sun dropped behind the Juarapas, Hector pulled the door open, held it there for Adolfo's entrance. Neither was as drunk as he might be.

I knew Adolfo's routine and braced myself. The others blew in the door, flapping their arms with the cold.

"The fire, boy," Adolfo demanded, reaching out to the top shelf. I bent to strike the match, listening to his beefy hand slapping back and forth in the dark, listening to the intake of breath.

"Mi venturosa uña!" he yelled.

"Your lucky nail?" Hector asked. "It is gone?"

The flames leapt on the hearth. Adolfo's hand dug into my shoulder, pulling me to my feet, turning me to face him.

"Boy?"

He did not expect a response. He would tell me what had happened, I would agree. His audience stood ready to hear the proclamation.

Instead, they heard my small voice. "The good sister," I said, surprised that I should speak at all, breathing in, trying to speak with certainty, trying to keep the register low. "It seemed she deserved at least one lucky nail."

The beating was not as bad as it might have been. He needed me to do the work. Only I knew his hands had grown weak with drink—too weak for good work. We all knew Adolfo could never face a night without his lucky nail. I should have held my tongue.

Still, it seemed my words, my daring, filled an empty space too long left hollow.

Back at Sister's grave, a flash of light from above, and I look up to Luna Madre, suddenly free from the clouds. I look down to the box, its dark knots scattered over the moonlit whiteness of the pine. Strange. Thin dark lines arc from the sides of the box to the center. No such lines were there when I built the box—only knots and slivers.

Of course. I lift one hand to my mouth, bear down, and pull a sliver. I feel nothing. I pull three more and wipe my hands on the serape. Hands will heal.

Luna Madre sends me light, and there is the shining silver glint—the very top of la venturosa uña—Adolfo's lucky nail. It glints in the corner above Sister's left shoulder. I fumble the hammer from my belt and run my hand over the newly smoothed ash of its handle. It balances well. Funny what one can do with some time, a discarded hammer head, a broken axe shaft, and a bit of skill.

The nail's head glints in the light of Luna Madre.

I can pull the nail, leaving the tiniest hole, just as I assembled the box, striking each nail perfectly, leaving no dent—not the slightest impression—just as I carefully sawed the sad, discarded pine. It is good to have skill. The smooth ash handle catches Luna Madre's light, and here I am, a boy with a hammer, with skills. A boy remembering Adolfo's story. Remembering.

Slowly, with certainty, I stand and slip the hammer back into my belt. Strange. It is no longer heavy.

Sister Lucia Maria, you may keep the nail.

Luna Madre throws a last flash of light to glint on the nail's silvery top as the first shovelful lands on the pine box. The next ones come with little effort.

The sand crunches lightly underfoot. They say the next village is a mere two days' walk. Luna Madre looks on from behind a thin veil of clouds. The village shovel makes a fine walking stick. The hammer swings at my belt.

This night may be cold, but not near as cold as I had thought.

C.S. Perryess taught middle school for years and now runs an academic day camp for middle schoolers at Cuesta College while maintaining a blog about words at Perryess.com. His short stories have appeared in *Highlights for Children, READ Magazine, Pangolin Papers, Eureka Literary Magazine, With,* and elsewhere. His work was anthologized in *In Short: How to Teach the Young Adult Short Story* (Heinemann 2005), and *Lay-Ups and Long Shots* (Darby Creek/Lerner, 2008). He's a Patti Gauch acolyte, a baker, a cyclist, and a musician, and he drives for the local food bank.

MOTHER-DAUGHTER LUNCHEON

Nonfiction by Debra Davis Hinkle

Mom is blessed with four daughters. Some women in our church don't have any children. So, Mom loans out her two older kids for the annual mother-daughter luncheon.

I am the third child, and Mom doesn't loan me or my little sister out.

I hate these functions because the food is weird. You can't tell what something is because it's mixed with a bunch of other stuff. The ladies seem proud of this food, and each dish seems to be a salad or casserole. Yuck. I like my plain peanut butter sandwiches, but I might be happy if I could see some meat without gravy.

After a few of these functions, I finally get smart and figure out how to get rid of the awful food before I'm forced to put it in my mouth. I practice my plan at home. I think I'm pretty good at scooping this pretend food into my imaginary purse. My last chore is to find the right purse, wide as a plate. My older sister lets me borrow hers.

The dreaded day arrives. All four girls in my family are in our church just a few blocks south of our house on the same street.

"Good afternoon, Betty," Mrs. Harriet says.

"Afternoon," Mom says. "My two oldest are sitting over there if you'd like to pick one for today and my two youngest are my guests."

"Who's going to borrow the other one?" Mrs. Harriet asked.

"Well, I promised Mrs. Otis one, too," Mom says. "But you're here now, so you get first choice." I like Mrs. Otis. She's the recess teacher at our school, and her son, Tony, is in my class.

"Betty, you might want to keep an eye on that one running …"

"Where are you going?" Mom asks.

"Bathroom!" I yell back up the stairs to Mom.

Ever since I was a little girl, the church bathroom has reeked like those strange toilets at campsites. It doesn't just stink, it makes me feel my Sunday dress is going to smell like a dirty diaper.

I usually hold my nose in the bathroom, but today I need both hands. The last thing I do is line my sister's purse with those dirty looking paper towels from the dispenser. I'm ready for the dreaded luncheon.

Mom stops my skipping in the hallway just outside the boy's bathroom and takes my hand and my little sister's and guides us to our places.

The meal is served in the large room downstairs. The big beige, plastic curtain that divides the room into two is pulled back. Our luncheon tables are in the center and the Sunday School classes occupy two of the three outside walls. Five or six rectangular tables are placed end to end, with bright white tablecloths on each. It looks sort of pretty, but the white linens will be covered in chunks of food soon enough. *I wonder if I could accidently on purpose spill some food.*

There aren't any pretty amber windows here like upstairs in the chapel or carved double doors or even beautiful wood doors. Just plain glass windows and three ugly, heavy, white doors with lots of dirty fingerprints on both sides and a metal bar across the middle on the inside. Two doors leading out to the asphalt parking lot, and one in a tiny Sunday school room that exits to the front side of the church.

The room is smelly from the food and the ladies' perfume. It's hot, too. The bathroom might smell better, and I know it's not as hot. Do I like smelly food mixed with gagging perfume or a dirty diaper smell? I always forget how horrible the chemical toilet smell is.

Here I go. *I wonder if hell has bad food, too.*

The chairs are brown, cold metal ones without padded seats. We are at the first table very near the second table. I'm sitting two places down from Mom. My little sister is between Mom and me. My two older sisters are sitting at the second table on the other side. They are just a hop, skip, and jump from us.

The food is served to me on a huge white plate. I feel like I'm going to gag, which happens to me when food is smelly or when I remember it tasted terrible the last time.

I know Mom talked to the lady who served my plate because I have only three things on it: meat of some kind, potatoes, and beans. I don't like gravy on my food, except for biscuits. Maybe Mom forgot to tell the lady *no greasy gravy* because my plate is oozing it. I put my head down to smell the food. Thank God, it's not quite as bad as the overall room smell. Maybe I can even force some down.

I take a bite of the mystery meat and it remains an unknown. A dry, overcooked piece of meat covered in greasy gravy. Out comes my savior, the purse.

I start to rearrange the "food" on my plate. I want it to look like I'm eating it. I scoot forward and place my purse on my knees at the edge of the table. I open my purse, and, as fast as I can, I slide the crap into it. I feel elated and oh-so-clever. I excuse myself and head for the bathroom, once again skipping but only the last twenty feet. I'm ready: garbage down the toilet and I reline the rescue purse.

Back at the table, I take my place, at ease for the first time. I look around and no one seems to be watching me. I smile at everyone like I'm happy to be here.

Refill time. This is going great. I'll probably only need three pursefuls. I'm a happy little girl.

I check to see if anyone is watching me. Coast clear; I excuse myself again and repeat the process only this time I put the icky food in the trash just in case the toilets stop working. I cover the food with more light brown paper towels. The towels are running low. But I know where the extra ones are in the cupboard just under the stairs next to the restroom. Purse lined, I'm skipping along the first hallway again. I slow down to a walk like nothing is wrong once I turn left into the short hallway that leads to the big room.

I take my seat for the third time. Too bad our seats are at the end of the first table. It sure would be easier to leave and sneak back if I was nearer the hallway. One more trip and my plate will be clean enough to get dessert.

I look around at the ladies and their daughters, real or borrowed, and they seem happy. They are eating this stuff and not complaining. I don't understand.

"Very good, Honey," Mom says. "Now just eat a little more."

I smile and nod at Mom. She seems proud of me; I sit up a little taller.

I eat a few very small bits of unidentified meat. The ritual begins— then I start moving the remaining food around and once again get closer to the table and open my purse. I scoop most of the remaining goop into my dump truck of a liberator, hoping to sneak away one last time.

Suddenly, I hear whispering voices and commotion. I dread looking up, and as I do, I lower my false savior and my head, looking out through my dark curly hair. I snap my purse shut.

I see my older sisters covering their laughter and some of the women elbowing their neighbors. Unfortunately, Mom sees and hears the commotion, too. She doesn't have to look left; she knows the problem is two chairs to the right of her. And she doesn't need the lady directly across from her to point at me. I don't either.

Mom's cheeks are turning red. I know she is embarrassed by my behavior, and I haven't gotten rid of all the food. Now I'm sitting in the middle of the commotion I caused. I wish I could disappear. *What do I do now?*

"What is that stuff in your purse?" Mom says in a soft, controlled voice.

"It's the awful food," I respond, honest to a fault. "I'm sorry, Mommy."

"I know, but you shouldn't throw food away. Don't do it again, Honey."

"Yes, Mommy."

I'm sure my mom thought she had averted any disaster that she could imagine. Now she probably wishes that I had sat in the chair next to her and my little sister in the one I was in.

I guess I won't be getting any dessert.

As it turns out, Mom knew better than to loan me out, but she let me get too far from her. I know Mom won't hurt me even if it was wrong to throw my food away. Mommy is never mean. It's enough punishment to know that I embarrassed her.

I'm keenly aware of the people, and it feels like everyone is still talking about me. Being "Christian ladies," they whisper and try not to point. Yeah. I don't feel elated or clever anymore. Now I feel fear.

Thank God it's a mother-daughter function, not a father-daughter one. He would have dragged me out of the church and beat the hell out of me and continued the beating after he drove the half mile to our house. I tremble at my next thought. *What if one of the ladies tells him or their husbands? Oh, no. I still might get a beating with his belt.*

I sure hope Mom knows how to fix this one. Maybe, I should consider where I am and pray. It can't hurt.

Dear God, I made a big booboo … and now I need your help. Please don't let Daddy hurt me again.

At bedtime, Mom brings a peanut butter sandwich wrapped in a paper napkin and a glass of milk to my room. She says, "Honey, after you finish the sandwich put the napkin in the glass and then put the glass under the bed, so your father won't see it. I love you, Debby."

Learn more about **Debra Davis Hinkle** at
DebraDavisHinkle.FridayNightWritersGroup.com.

SPRING TRIP TO THE LAKE

Poetry by Nancy R. Yang

the rented house on the water
its iron statue of a horse on the lawn
and forget-me-nots scattered like glitter
the freeway in the distance is a white whir.

The ride in the car for barbecue, windows down
so everyone can see my face. Like the little boys
turning their faces up like dogs in the side mirror,
hair blowing like the wheat in fields we pass.

I'm king of the world! they yell to the wheat-growing sun,
reaching for a sweet morsel of childhood, grabbing
on to stay forever, warmth in me like an early hot flash,
the moment a taste of salt on my tongue—

it will pass quickly. The ride
back, the kids beg us to roll the windows down
again, we take the long route into the sunset. *Fast!*
the week will go by, the clothes I'll fold will gather
again, arrange into the suitcase my curling iron.

Sometimes, people think
they'll take the cotton candy and funnel cakes home,
recreate sugar so sweet in a sea of Tuesdays.

We'll wave goodbye to the show jumping horse
on our way towards home we touch rust on the saddle of this day,
we see it spreading to its mane.

Father says to bow our heads

Poetry by Nancy R. Yang

Sometimes when I fret I see
sugar chalk on malted chocolate, in dreams,
hidden prizes in grass, bunnies and bibles,
long altar calls: *Lord, I come*
over and over my young stomach rumbles
while Mom holds the red-covered hymnal
down so I see, so I sing along:
watermelon, watermelon, deviled eggs,
ham still untouched, the centerpiece,
still-to-come pleasantries, more prayers
from the table's head—Dad or the pastor
Mom invited in his tan coat, pale pink tie,
I'll hold my brother's hand,
close my eyes, look focused: *Please*
make this fast, I'm so hungry, I'll be good.
I'll fill up, ask to be excused and vanish
down to Indian Creek and hum to myself,
stay a long time, staring at the running water
over the brown rocks, like a vein through the body
of the earth in its own worship, flowing
all the way to far—as far away as a lifetime—
to the sea.

ROSES AND HONEYSUCKLE

Poetry by Nancy R. Yang

The afternoon's calm rhythmic clicking, the chime
the grandfather clock at Nana's
the hall dark and scary like a tunnel
the back room, the rocking horse
a fall to the hardwood floor,
my nosebleed. Nana's warmth,
my head near hers as the pain waned.

The memory blends of South Carolina,
the toothache I had that day, cherry medicine
the open window, soft chirps
the smell of honeysuckle
from beneath the sill where I'd help, learn
from Grandma when she'd water the flowers—
peace that afternoon, like my soul
had been told a secret.

I notice now when the washer stops
the television is off, no one is around
I can hear the flow of blood
inside my ears, like a whisper from Aunt Virginia
saying *all we really need to know*—
I can almost grasp it again
like it's coming in through the screen,
but only a touch, for now.

Nancy R. Yang is an educator and MFA candidate in creative writing at Pacific University. A long-time transplant to California, she grew up in Georgia and South Carolina, where her love of art was formed. Her poems have appeared in *Poetry South*, *Willows Wept Review*, and *Aura Literary Arts Review*, among others.

AN ARRANGED MARRIAGE

Fiction by Tom Brauner

Walking down the path into their lush back yard, gray pea-gravel crunching under his feet, Rex decides that today is the day to discuss his plan with Patricia. He has just returned from his appointment with his oncologist. Dr. Bell had stated that nothing remained in his treatment armamentarium; chemo, radiation, surgery had all failed. Rex, confronting this seemingly unassailable problem, feels an urgent need to take action in the same way he built his business—by assessing problems and finding an immediate remedy.

The idea has been percolating for a few months now, and while he is quite certain how Patricia will react when he sits down to discuss it with her, he feels convinced that this is the best option. Every trait he feels he has in such limited supply—kindness, empathy, warmth—Patricia has in abundance. She will hear the latest news from Dr. Bell, and her own needs will come a distant second to his. For once, he does not want this to happen.

He finds her at the end of the path, expectantly waiting for him on the patio swing at the bottom of the yard, her worry impossible to disguise. He hadn't wanted her to come to the appointment with Dr. Bell because … he wasn't sure he could hear the report and watch his wife's face at the same time. Now he wishes Patricia *had* come so he didn't have to have this part of the conversation. Rex sits down next to her and, before she can ask, volunteers the news.

"Dr. Bell says there are no more options, Patty. We're on the last leg of the flight with no place to land." When he'd retired from the business, Rex had decided he would finally learn to fly, realizing a boyhood dream. He never tires of flying metaphors, although Patricia had tired of them almost immediately.

Her voice quavers and catches. "How long does he think, Rex?"

"Two months … plus or minus."

She begins to cry, and he moves closer to her, close enough to smell the scent of her hair and the Chanel perfume she so loves, putting his arm around her and pulling her tight to him. His sweet girl; what she saw in him he never understood, but he is so glad she saw it. Fifty-five years. The time had flown and now he was going to fly away from her, too. He brushes water out of his eyes with the back of his sleeve, then uses the same sleeve to gently brush some of the tears from Patty's cheeks. *When you start the flight together, you hope for clear skies the whole way.* He didn't say this out loud of course. She would have just rolled her eyes and cried harder.

The next afternoon, Rex asks Patricia to come sit outside with him. The Santa Barbara day is sunny and warm, and the poppies are in bloom in her bee-friendly habitat. He always went along for the ride with that sort of stuff. It was the kind of thing that Patricia thought through carefully before she took action. The beautiful way it always turned out stunned him when he took the time to notice.

They had met during the early years of his business, American Staple. After he'd returned from Vietnam, Rex had studied chemistry and business at Cal State Northridge. In a late-night laboratory mistake, he created an adhesive that lightly bonded metal to metal. After graduation, he worked on possible applications until he hit upon the idea of using it to adhere individual staples together. It ended up being the cornerstone of his business.

As the company began to grow, Rex was swamped with work. He placed a help-wanted ad for a secretary in The Santa Clarita Valley Signal. He had already gone through several desultory interviews (*Where was their damn work ethic?*) when Patricia came in to apply for the position. He liked her no-nonsense style and the fact she had managed the front office for her dad's tool-and-die shop since she was in middle school. And Patricia *was* easy on the eyes, which was an acceptable thing to say in those days. Rex offered her the job on the spot. He asked her to marry him three months after he hired her—with the understanding they would continue to work together. She had said yes to both propositions.

American Staple would not have taken root and blossomed without their complementary talents. Rex was good at manufacturing and Patricia was a genius with people. They were as completely intertwined as two partners could be.

Three months, two years, then suddenly twenty years, and finally—in what was surely only another blink of an eye—fifty-five years together. They'd created a thriving business, raised three great boys (mostly Patricia's doing, he frequently declared) and now, as Rex sees it, his cancer has thrown a spanner in the works. He desperately wants to assure Patty's happiness after he is gone.

"So, I've been doing some thinking," he begins.

"Of course you have," she says. "That's what you do." Her eyes were puffy and red-rimmed from crying.

"How would you feel about screening some candidates for my replacement?"

Her mouth opens and contorts into various shapes, but no words come out. She gets up to leave and Rex pulls her back.

"Hold on a second, Patty. Hear me out. You know I'm a first-rate problem-solver."

Patricia's cheeks were now becoming as red as her eyes. "Don't you think that maybe this is not *your* problem to solve, Rex, and that maybe this isn't the time to have such a ridiculous conversation?"

"Look, Patty, there isn't much time … I don't have much time *left*. You're the only thing I worry about now. I'm on the final glide path— sorry, that just came out—but you're in great physical shape, you're still beautiful, you have who knows how many good years left."

"Rex, this is crazy. We're both upset, but I don't want to have this discussion now or tomorrow, or *ever* for that matter."

"Patty, I love you. You've always been the best part of my life. My timing may be lousy, but I know you're happiest with other people around. That is who *you* are."

"I have friends for that, Rexford."

He knew she was mad when she used his whole name, but he would not—could not—relent. "You need your own person, Sweetheart. We both know it."

"Discussion ended, case closed," and with that Patricia rises and walks into the house.

But Rex doesn't close cases quite *that* easily.

Three days later at the breakfast table, Patricia finds the ***From the Desk of Rexford Powers*** memo card beside her coffee cup. In Rex's perfect printing he had written in pencil (as if it might be subject to revision):

My Top Three Candidates for the Job

Jack Bluther

Arthur Tamblin

Remy Charles

She pours herself a cup of coffee and sighs. She knows that Rex is feeling untethered and out of control and is seeking a way to take care of her. But how (for the thousandth time) can she get him to understand that people need to *feel* things and *deal* with their feelings before solving a problem? Patricia thinks back to all the things they had accomplished together, but she knows that *this* problem has no solution. She can certainly be angry with Rex—she'd often felt the heat of that emotion during the first ten years of their marriage. But eventually, she saw beneath the surface and understood that he was a good man who always, in his way, thought that he was putting her first. This is another instance of that fundamental goodness, and she adores him for that. *But Jesus, can't he just let me be sad?*

She glances at the names on the card and is about to crumple it up when she thinks better of it. As always, it provides insight into the man she married and for that alone it has value. So here were her well-meaning husband's picks for her future companion: Jack Bluther, Arthur Tamblin, and Remy Charles. She knows all three men, of course. Now as she attempts to think like Rex, Patricia mulls over how he has selected them.

Jack and Carol Bluther had been their closest friends as a couple. Rex had met Jack in the service and so they shared a long friendship. Carol quickly came to be Patricia's best friend. The couples had traveled together, had alternated family Thanksgiving holidays for decades, had been together when one of the Bluther's then-teenage sons had almost died in a car accident. Patricia and Rex had also supported the couple when Carol was diagnosed with breast cancer, had gone into remission for ten years, and then suddenly and unexpectedly died within a few months of a recurrence. That was three years ago. Now, despite his loss, Jack maintains a lightness and optimism that Patricia admires. Not hard to see how Rex has settled on Jack.

Arthur Tamblin was Rex's flying instructor. He had retired as a military pilot and then decided he didn't want to work for an airline. Arthur wanted to share his love of flying with others, that awesome joy of seeing the world uniquely from a thousand feet above the earth. He had joined them for dinner on several occasions, and they invariably shared an evening filled with nice wine and laughter. Arthur was a raconteur but felt no need to dominate the conversation; he could listen, and he was smart and undeniably handsome. Patricia wasn't sure if he, too, specialized in flying metaphors, but if so, he must only deploy them in an airplane cockpit.

Of the three men, Patricia thinks Remy Charles is the outlier. He is the diametric opposite of Rex. Remy Charles, with his lilting French accent and electric blue eyes. When Carol Bluther was first diagnosed with breast cancer, she'd seen Remy for therapy to manage the roller-coaster experience of the cancer treatments and the welter of emotions she faced. Remy Charles was there again at the end of her life, sitting with Jack and his family and with Patricia and Rex when they visited Carol in her home during hospice. Remy was born outside of Paris and came to the States for college. Patricia doubts that it is the accent or French pedigree that places him on Rex's list. She wonders how Remy even made it *onto* Rex's list.

She folds the card once and puts it in her jacket pocket before walking out into the back garden. Despite herself, Patricia smiles. Rex is certainly a piece of work, but he is *her* piece of work, and she feels grateful—most of the time.

Here is how Rex came up with the list. He thinks of it like a football draft: each person can fill a specific position—or in this case a function—he feels Patty might need once he is gone.

Jack Bluther. Jack is his lifelong friend, and Rex knows how highly Patty regards him. Frankly, both of them need a mate, and the takeoff and landing should be pretty smooth.

Arthur Tamblin. Handsome, funny, adventurous. Most importantly, he once pointed out how lucky Rex was to find a girl like Patty. Rex *will* have to give Arthur a head's up about the flying metaphors and that Patty hates to be called a girl.

Remy Charles. Remy is really Rex's first choice, which is why he lists him last, to give Patty a little something extra to chew on. When he was thinking about the kind of person Patty needed, he realized that the man should be well-evolved and, perhaps more than anything, a man quite different from Rex. He wants Patty to have the experience of being with someone completely unlike him, not because of any jealousy on his part, but because she deserves someone who can take care of *her* emotionally for a change rather than he other way around. This is going to be a hard sell, though. Patty is pretty set in her ways.

The week after he places the memo beside her coffee cup, Patricia comes out to the garden to find Rex sitting on the bench looking at their wedding album.

"I haven't looked at these since we got married." He turns a page. "You were awful pretty." He closes the book and gazes up at her.

She sits beside him as her cheeks flush with color, an ineffable spark between them still.

Rex watches a hummingbird flit around the red and yellow feeder.

"I was thinking about a party, sort of a Last Waltz kind of thing."

Patricia studies him.

"I can say my goodbyes. Just the most important people."

The recognition dawns. "Ah yes, I see. The band could include Jack, Arthur, and maybe Remy? Sort of an *audition*? You could stroll around, whisper your plan to the boys?"

"Okay, okay. I see you don't like it."

"Wearing yourself out because you can't let go of your crazy idea? Nope, I don't like it."

She looks out at the garden. "You can't control this, Rex. You're scared just like *I'm* scared, but not for the same reasons. You're scared because you want to know how it turns out. I'm scared because I know how hard it's going to get."

They both watch for a long time as the hummingbird dips its slender beak into the feeder's nectar.

"I never could have guessed how good it would all turn out, –Patty— except for this last part."

"Just another way that you and I are different, Rex. I *liked* not knowing how it would turn out."

The hummingbird finally flies away.

Patricia gently takes his hand. "There will always be some mystery, Rex."

They look at each other, as if young lovers once again, and kiss.

Eventually though, Rex can't help himself and says, "Still, a man should have a plan."

As it happens, the universe is unmoved that Rex is fast approaching the end of his runway and wants to have a plan for Patricia. Ten days after their conversation in the garden, he can hardly rise from the bed. He spikes a fever that won't remit, and the pain nearly crushes him. They call in hospice care, but Patty won't leave his side, sitting or lying beside him around the clock.

"I'd like to go into the garden," he rasps one day near the end.

Patty and the hospice nurse, William, load him into the wheelchair, and Patty pushes him through the bedroom sliders that lead outside. Rex feels the chill in the air as summer passes the baton to autumn. Patty parks him beside the bench near the hummingbird feeder. She watches him with a mixture of love and dread as he struggles to catch his breath, just the act of being wheeled here having exacted a toll.

Finally, he says, "Patty, I wanted to say my goodbyes to a lot of people, but there's no time now. It's moving too fast."

Rex pants and his eyes are teary. Patricia sits down on the bench beside his wheelchair, gently laying her head on his shoulder.

"I don't care if you end up with one of those guys on my list. You don't need my help to find someone. I was just desperate to know he'd be a good one."

She takes a long moment, composes herself, and finally says to him gently, "It's enough that I've been with a good one my whole life, Rex."

They hold each other tenderly, he in his wheelchair and she on the bench, and cry for a long time.

Finally, he says, "I'm so sorry to leave you, Sweetheart, but I'm very happy you were my co-pilot on this flight."

Patty just cries harder.

Three weeks later, surrounded by Patricia and their boys, Rex takes one final breath, and his essence wings skyward, charting a course for parts unknown.

More than five hundred people attend the funeral at Our Lady of Sorrows. The eulogies sparkle, eliciting both laughter and tears. They capture a man who thought he wasn't very good with people but who had, in fact, left an indelible mark on almost everyone. Employees of American Staple get up to speak, thanking Rex—and Patricia—for giving them the chance at jobs that were not in the Santa Barbara fields. Jack Bluther calls Rex a "great man" and talks about how he learned to be a good man by watching his friend day after day. His sons speak, and the hospice nurse, William, gets up and talks about the final hours with "Rex and his amazing family." Patricia hears the emotion in their voices and the love in their words and feels lucky that Rexford Powers had been *hers*.

And, perhaps not surprisingly, the three men listed on Rex's prophetic notecard each played a major role in the weeks leading up to, and in the months following, Rex's death.

Remy Charles is still working a few days each week as a hospice therapist when the request comes in to visit Rex and Patricia at their home. He remembers them both well, and despite all his experience, is startled when he contrasts his memory of the vital Rex with the cadaverous man he finds lying in the hospital bed in the living room. Nonetheless, Rex reaches for his hand and, smiling beatifically, says, "I'm so glad they sent *you*." Remy comes every day, leaving only when Rex gives him the sign. Patricia finds the Frenchman's warmth and care reassuring and asks Remy to be in the room with her and her family in the waning hours of Rex's life. He is there when Rex takes his last breath.

Fittingly, Rex had made a request to have Arthur Tamblin take Patricia up in a Cessna 182, his favorite airplane, to spread his ashes several thousand feet above the Santa Ynez Mountains. Patricia talks about Rex's late-in-life love affair with flying, and Arthur declares that it was his love for *her* that Rex had always mentioned. "He wore that on his sleeve, Patricia." She is pleased to hear this from Arthur. She is also pleased that throughout the flight he uses not a single flying metaphor.

Jack Bluther is steadfast and calm, not only speaking at the funeral, but also clairvoyantly dropping in whenever Patricia most needs someone to talk to. They reminisce about their mates and how lonely they feel without them. They share a deep understanding of what they each had and an abiding grief at what each has lost.

They are worthy men all, but quite unexpectedly Patty finds herself drawn to someone not on Rex's list. She is surprised and then pleased by this recognition. In the years ahead, she will sometimes gaze skyward and smile.

Sometimes love favors an alternate flight plan.

<hr>

Tom Brauner has a Doctorate in Clinical Social Work and for many years worked with neuro-divergent children and their families, as well as with individuals and couples in private practice. He has always loved books and literature. After retiring in 2023, he has finally found the time to write.

MELISSA

Nonfiction by Heather Campbell

I was afraid to speak to you at the start. You were a writer, I was not. You were accomplished, I was not. People tend to lay down different aspects of themselves, depending on who they are with, but you were always beautifully you. You were kind and thoughtful, and you made me change the way I thought about myself. You were the bridge between my past and the me that could have been, the me that maybe still could be.

We met online at a writing conference. You were my teacher for one week. The pandemic forced us into creative replacements for life, and we watched each other on small rectangular screens for three hours a day. Before I met you, and for as long as I can remember, I'd write a few lines, and then crumple them up and throw them away. I was too afraid to write. I thought to even attempt it was gratuitous, and anytime I tried, I was filled with shame. That time when we were not allowed to leave our homes was awful, but it taught me that most things don't really matter as much as you think they do. With your encouragement, I wrote. I pretended *I* was Virginia Woolf, putting rocks in *my* pockets before stepping into the River Ouse.

During our class you gave us prompts and asked us to write for ten minutes. Once we finished, we read aloud to each other. I watched your face as I shared, wondering if I'd pleased you. As I read on our second day, I saw your head tilt and your eyes soften. I held my breath as you wondered aloud, "People don't usually do that in ten minutes." A flush of heat came over me as I took your kind words in. It felt as if in that moment you picked up the pieces of my broken childhood and placed them back together.

After the class ended, I was afraid I would never hear your voice or your careful choice of words again. In a moment of panic, I asked your teaching assistant for your email address. She sent it to me the same day, and I wrote to you that afternoon.

In your first message you wrote, "I am so glad you reached out, if you hadn't, I was going to contact you, to tell you how much I liked the work you did and see if there was anything I could do to help." I nearly cried.

The first time we spoke, just the two of us, I was so nervous I nearly didn't answer the phone, but I knew this might be my only chance, and I took a deep breath, picked up the phone and said, "Hello."

You said you'd like to meet in person. You asked, "Would that be ok?" It had to be in the late afternoon or evening. Anything before three o'clock in the afternoon was no good. I didn't understand, but I didn't ask why. I would have met you outside Penn Station at midnight if you'd asked. But you chose a French café. It became our place.

When we first met, I was still too worried to sit inside, and we bundled and shivered as we sipped our cappuccinos, and you crunched the ice left from the diet soda you always ordered. During our first meeting, you explained that the ice chips relieved the pain from the sores the chemo left behind. You didn't feel well some days. Afternoons were your best bet. You told me because you didn't want me to think it was me if you had to cancel at the last minute. You told me you always wanted to see me when you were able. You looked forward to it. I know I blushed then.

One week after we finished our cappuccinos, I read to you about the time my mother blamed me for her latest suicide attempt. "My brother called me that night to say they had finally found our mother in some cheap midtown hotel. I wondered if she had a view of Times Square, one whose lights lit up her room even when the curtains were drawn. The police kicked down the door, dragged her out, and strapped her to a gurney. The sirens blared all the way to Bellevue where she had her stomach pumped, my father by her side."

You told me I was raised by wolves, and I laughed, but we both knew it was true. You wondered what things would have been like if my childhood had been different. I shifted uncomfortably and said it probably wasn't useful for me to think about that. Too many people are consumed by their resentments.

Sometimes I worried that my past was the only reason you spent time with me. You read my stories. You knew they were sad. I was afraid you were only there at that café because you pitied me. I also worried that I was in that café because I was looking for a mother. You didn't have children. Maybe we needed each other. But I tried to push those feelings away because they were dark and uncomfortable. You said you wanted to read what I wrote. I wasn't very disciplined, I explained. You said we should meet every Thursday afternoon at four o'clock so that I would not stop writing. It was the greatest kindness I have ever been given. Why couldn't I just leave it at that? I tried hard not to look at you as my mother, as though I were some stray lost bird fallen out of her nest, but it wasn't easy.

We didn't always eat when we were at our café, but when we did, you ordered a side of ratatouille. It did not look good to me, but you once told me that if there were kibble for humans, you'd buy it, and then the ratatouille made more sense. The day we ordered food for the first time, I ordered escargot, and you seemed pleased. It felt good to have your proud eyes looking at me. I laughed and said, "It was nothing, the dish is really just a vehicle for butter."

This made you happier. "That's just what my boyfriend says!"

You loved your boyfriend very much. You had been together for sixteen years and you used words like *enthralled* and *rapt* and your eyes did a melty sort of thing when you talked about him. I was amazed. I did not know these feelings were possible after sixteen years. You shared two dogs, your Labrador retriever and your mother's standard poodle who you inherited when she passed away. I met your Labrador one day when we were at our café. He was walking by with the dog walker, and they came over to say hello. I got down low and cooed to the dog so he would love me as much as I loved you. I wanted to have a love in common. I remember you were surprised by how much he seemed to like me, and I was glad, but I was also worried that I was trying too hard and that you would notice.

It was cold out and finally one week I said it was okay to sit inside. You were more at ease with the state of the world than I was, and the other patrons did not bother you. I always got there first and tried to find a table away from others. I hated when people sat too close to us. It was four o'clock. Why was anyone else there? I wanted them to leave. You were sick enough already. I did not want you to catch what they might have.

The café was small, and the kitchen was open, so our clothes always smelled like hot butter when we left. The tables were dark wood and tacky, a reminder to keep my elbows off the table. Sometimes the kitchen smoke burned my eyes. "Read me your pages," you'd say. You always asked me to read aloud. You never took the pages in your hands.

I read to you, worried that I would disappoint you, worried that you'd come to think this was all a waste of your time.

But then you asked me to read a second time. "I'd like to hear it again if that's okay?" I'd barely made it through the first read, my face was flushed, but I couldn't say no. I tried to breathe as I began again.

You always wore a beautiful scarf and often a crisp white shirt. I invariably dressed for you. I wanted to look like someone that you wanted to be sitting with in a French café every Thursday at four o'clock.

One rainy Thursday the music was too loud. "I can't hear you reading," you said. I got up and asked them to turn the music down a little, please. I hoped very much that you would be impressed by my bravery.

Before I read to you each week, we'd share parts of our lives. I was on the edge of my seat as I listened to stories about your best friend, the poet, and your dear friend who was ninety-three and said anything she liked. You had plans for us all to meet and to see a film together, maybe on a

Tuesday afternoon. I loved when you made plans for us that were in the future. Sometimes you told me about people in your life who were unkind. Only once did you mention some of your accomplishments, and it was in defiance of them that you whispered. "Well I did write two best sellers … translated into dozens of languages. Coppola bought my film rights! Sold over a million and a half copies. Still, they act like I have no business being at their dinner party."

If only I'd been in the room. What I would have told them about how to behave kindly to others. But you just walked away. Your absence was their great loss. These stories allowed me to try the same. It turns out saying "no more, thank you very much" to those who are unkind frees up quite a bit of time.

One week you called moments before we were to meet and said you were in too much pain. You could not make it.

"That's all right. Please don't worry," I said.

"Unless you want to come here, to me," you suggested.

My heart skipped a beat. To your home? I asked.

"Only if you're comfortable," you said.

I am. I am. I am. I told the doorman who I was there to see, and he smiled as I entered your elevator. I knocked on your door and then you were there framed in orange. I did not know what to expect, but I loved knowing that about you … that you would paint your walls orange.

"Come in," you said. You wrapped a blanket around your shoulders and took the armchair and I the couch. You offered me a soda. "It's the good kind," you said. I declined and you got yourself one. When you came back you were holding a Schweppes diet ginger ale in a small glass jar and this made me smile. "I never let anyone into my home," you told me. "As you can see it's sort of like the inside of a drawer." I very much liked this description, and I tried to take in as much of the room as I could without being rude. I could have stayed in there all day, turning over every object in my hands. That night you gave me a copy of *The Friend*. "I have my own copy and I found this in the free book depository of my building, so please don't worry about giving it back to me," you said. The book was brand new, and I wondered whether you'd bought it for me but didn't want to say.

I started the book that night and was pulled through the story of a woman who loses her friend and writing mentor to suicide. After her mentor dies, the narrator adopts the deceased's beloved Great Dane, Apollo, who no one else will take in. She develops an unusual relationship with Apollo, and it seemed to me that the woman talks to him as if he were the lost mentor. She lives in New York City and is not allowed to have dogs in her apartment, never mind a Great Dane, and so she almost loses her home and arguably her mind as she unravels. Well the back of the book describes her as unraveling, but I didn't really agree with that. I thought she seemed perfectly sane. I tried not to read too deeply into the plot. You liked the book. You gave me a found copy. Simple. But were you going to give me your dog one day?

Four months before I met you I was locked in my house, like much of the world. I left the city with my family for a home with a yard and a pond. When we first pulled up that day in March I had a plant on my lap because I knew that we were going to be there for a while. The first thing I noticed were two geese in the yard. My five-year-old daughter chased them back into the pond each day because I told her that I did not like them on our grass.

When I was young, my grandfather used to shoo the geese off his yard and back into the lake near their home. "If I had a gun, I'd shoot them," he'd say. I was horrified … shoot them for making a mess on his lawn? But it did not stop me from shooing those geese off my own lawn those days in March, although I didn't *think* I would ever shoot them.

But one day the geese did not run away. They came straight for my daughter. I ran screaming from the kitchen, slippers in hand, arms flapping wildly. I tried to look big, like someone once told me to do if I saw a bear. The geese ran back into the pond, and my terrified daughter collapsed into my arms.

Within the week the geese had six babies. Only then did it occur to me why they were there. Every morning I looked out my window as the six goslings floated round and round after their mother, who sometimes led them in a row up onto our yard to peck at the ground. They were only there for a few days, and then suddenly the babies were gone. The parents remained, but the babies were gone. A hawk? someone suggested. I couldn't bear it. The parents stayed a couple more days and then they too left us all alone.

The summer after we met, I went back to the writing conference where we first met. We were supposed to go together, this time in person, but you were too sick to go, and you urged me to go on without you. I was alone at dinner one night after my second day of class when you messaged. *I am at our place*, you told me. *I am imagining you sitting across from me.* You had just gotten back from the hospital after having your blood drawn. I knew you were tired, but you still asked about me. *How do you feel? Have you made any friends yet? It can feel quite lonesome at the beginning. I can't wait to see what you come up with. I wish I were there with you.*

That was the last message I got from you. Your boyfriend told me you kept thinking you'd get strong enough soon to call me yourself. "Don't call her. She doesn't have to come. I'll see her soon," she told him. He was so sorry when he called that morning. I was sorry too. I knew how hard it must have been for him, your rapt love.

Sometimes it feels like a hawk took you. You were here for a moment. You were unexpected and lovely and terrifying because I didn't think I'd ever have someone like you to love. I didn't know that I deserved it, but you assured me that I did, and I had to believe you. I believed everything about you.

I went walking after I got the news, reflecting on that short year we had together. I thought back to one talk in particular, when we discussed the problems I had with memoir. How can we write about what we are in? How do we know when we are changed enough to make the story worth putting on the page? You smiled and said kindly, "Just keep going, you don't need to worry about that now."

Every year two geese arrive at the pond in mid-March and stay a while. I imagine it is the same geese, but I have not seen goslings since that first year. One night I sat at the edge of the pond thinking of you. I was watching the geese and considering the absence of their children when a blue heron glided down and settled beside them in the still, dark water. I watched it silently and realized that a story doesn't have to end to write about it. I don't really know the story of the geese, but here I was, year after year, watching it begin anew.

Heather Campbell is a writer living in New York City. Her work has been published in *HerStry* and *The Coachella Review*, and she is honored to be included in the current issue of *The NightWriter Review*. You can follow her on Instagram at @hacwrites.

DOWN A HOLE

Poetry by Scott Dalgarno

for Lucie Brock-Broido

When I was very young every once in a while there'd be a black-n-white report on television of some child that had fallen down a well or who had gotten stuck in an impossible crevice somewhere deep in the earth and all day and half the night it would go on while regular programing would be interrupted and people would watch for a while and then go on about their business but their thoughts would be with the child way down in that hole as if it were their niece or their son or themselves—you'd be out at some public event or you'd be shopping and your mother would ask if anyone knew the latest on the child and we would all suddenly just for a day be one human family; then in the night sitting on the floor in your pajamas you'd be watching as the news people searched awkwardly for something new to say when finally the announcer's voice would rise and "Look!" said your sister pointing as someone would lift the child out dazed by the quartz lights trembling limp and thousands in the country would be bawling their 1950s heads –off—even your father.

in the only tall grass left to mow miguel ignacio
naps after taking his lunch

Poetry by Scott Dalgarno

it's May and he's working ahead of the summer wildfires ahead of june bugs ahead of palm trees springing up in Alaska ahead of the next insurrection ahead of a mile-wide asteroid ahead of the Big One in California ahead of the little one his fiancée is expecting ahead of his first heart attack and the Second Coming ahead of Memorial Day which will be his last since on the next the woman he will never marry will come to the cemetery early with their baby in order to trim the grass around his marker with kitchen scissors, a shallow marker that will say he lived gently, left hardly a mark

LETTER TO OUR ADORABLE ZYGOTE
WHO WENT UNREALIZED

Poetry by Scott Dalgarno

I'm sure you'd have been a pistol.
You'd be eleven now, just beginning
to tell me you hate me. So bummed,
I never got to bounce you
on my knee.
I was already heels-over-head in love
with you
like you might have been
had you lived. We could have been
two shirts on one hanger.
Finally my life was NOT defined
by all my worst –moments—
throwing up on that ferris wheel,
telling your mother how beautiful
her sister was.
I'm such a failure. I mean,
even a lawn sprinkler
can make a rainbow.
Walking my despair
around the block here
the goddamn neighborhood
looks like hell: tipped garbage
bins, broken strollers, used condoms.
Your not being here
is everywhere.

Scott Dalgarno counts himself fortunate to have seen his poems in *APR*, *The Yale Review*, *The Antioch Review*, *Bellevue Literary Review*, *Pilgrimage Magazine*, *America*, *Cagibi*, and *The Oregonian*. His poem "Small Pleasures" placed second in the 2024 Oregon Poetry Association Prose Poem contest. His volume, *Third-Class Relics*, was a finalist for the 2024 Sally Albiso Poetry Book Award and will be published by MoonPath Press in 2025. He lives among firs and dogwoods near Portland, Oregon, where he works for the resistance.

THE ESSENCE

Fiction by Christine Ahern

"The Essence" is an Editor's Choice selection for this issue.

Sophia brought the cinnamon stick to her nose. Would this be it? Was this where she would find him? She closed her eyes and saw the image of Robert rolling out pie crust dough. She pictured his hands as they chopped and mixed and kneaded and powdered. Cakes and cookies, pastries and pies. The smell of the cinnamon skimmed along the surface of her brain. But cinnamon wasn't it. It wasn't what she was searching for. The nutmeg she had put in her coffee and sprinkled on her yogurt that morning was closer. But not it. The scent of cream, sugar, flour, butter, mint. All close. So close. But not it.

"Sophia." Her mother sat next to her. She put a sprig of mint to her nose. "You are not going to find Robert hidden somewhere, in something. He's gone."

"Some part of him still exists. He told me. The essence of him is somewhere."

For weeks after Robert died, she had wandered around the house and garden looking for the shadow of him. She had turned on favorite music, then sat in silence listening for the sound of him. She had lain in their bed, rolled on their sheets, showered in their shower, searching for the feel of him. Then, one foggy morning filled with the smell of damp earth and air, she realized she needed to look for him in a scent. The part of the brain that registers smell is closest to the part of the brain that holds memory. She knew this. So, she concluded, she would find the essence of Robert in a scent.

"He told me to look for him." Sophia ran her hands through the mint then stepped to the cabinet above the stove. That cabinet held his spices. And they were *his* spices. The kitchen was *his* domain. She wondered suddenly, as she looked around, why she even considered looking for him anywhere other than the kitchen. She laughed. "I don't know what I was thinking," she said as she turned back to her mother.

"You were thinking that you missed him." Margaret smiled at her with a look of relief that Sophia wasn't sure how to interpret. "And, now that you have seen that this search of yours is only causing you more pain, I hope we can move on to talking about the decisions you need to make. About the house, the cars . . ."

Sophia shook her head. Her mother didn't get it. This search of hers was the all of her days. It was the totality of her life. She would find him.

"Mom, why don't you go home. I'm okay. I'm doing fine. I'm not losing my mind, like you and Rosie imagine. It's only been two months. I think I am entitled to mourn however I need to mourn for at least two months. Don't you?"

Margaret shrugged her sweater to her shoulders and stood from the table. "Your sister and I are just worried about you. It was all so sudden, after all. So tragically sudden."

"Yes, it was. Tragically sudden. And tragically sad. Like everyone assured me they were heartbrokenly aware of in all the cards and texts and calls. But Mom," she took Margaret's hand, "at least I got to say goodbye. And he got to say goodbye to me. That was a gift."

Margaret removed her hand and patted Sophia's face. "You tell me, then. You tell me when you are ready to take the next step."

Her mother's hand smelled of mint. A lovely scent. But not it.

The accident that took Robert from her was one of those freak things, as they say. One of those things that wasn't supposed to happen. Not to Robert. Not to her. Not at their young age. Not when they were just beginning. She got the call while she was at work. She made it to the ER just in time, as they say. She ran to his side and took his face in her hands and saw him open his eyes for the last time. She made it just in time to see life leave his body, in time to hear him whisper his last words: "Look for me."

At first she thought maybe he meant to look for him in the next life, on another celestial plain, in her dreams. She decided, no, he meant something tangible. Because he was who he was, and he knew she knew him to be who he was. A practical man. Robert believed in what he could see, feel, and touch. And smell.

Sophia walked her mother to the door. "Tell Rosie I will call her when I'm ready to box up his things. I know she doesn't think I should do it alone, and I appreciate that. Tell her I promise not to do it alone."

Actually, Sophia had already started emptying Robert's closet and removing his things from the bathroom. She had removed them in her search for him, and when she didn't find him, she saw no point in putting it all back. She folded the clothes from his closet and put them and his toiletries in suitcases. Like she was packing him for a trip. And in a way, she thought, she was. The final trip. But she would leave the rest, for Rosie. Evidently Rosie needed closure, as they say. She needed to be part of Sophia's grieving. She needed to be there for her. Sophia could give her that.

As she passed through the living room to the kitchen, Sophia ran her hand along the books in the bookcase. Some hers. Some his. Some theirs. She pulled out the bread baking book Robert's grandmother had left to him. She held it to her heart. Opened it and leafed through the pages. She held it to her nose and inhaled. She inhaled the memory of his grandmother, whom she had grown to love in the short time she had known her. This book held her essence. She had always felt it. So, she knew it was possible for the essence of someone to be held in an inanimate object. As long as that object also held love, she thought. She slid the book back into its home among the other books and continued to the kitchen.

She stood in the dim light. Then she began to pull out drawers, one at a time. She opened and looked. She moved things around a bit, imagining that she was shuffling the scents, then bent to inhale. To her surprise each drawer held its own specific smell. One smelled slightly of wood, one of spices, one metallic. She opened cabinets, one at a time, and stirred up those smells. Soon her head was too full. Full of scents and thoughts. Of memories. Of longing and aching. Finally, she slid to the floor and leaned against the stove. Opposite the stove was the cabinet where Robert kept his pie pans and cookie sheets. His loaf pans and Bundt pan. She crawled across the floor and slowly opened it. The pans were stacked neatly, by size and type. All the Pyrex together, stacked large to small. All the stainless steel and aluminum, resting neatly inside each other. The Corning Ware casserole dishes Robert had inherited from his grandmother, stacked so that the flower edging and ivy trim showed. She crossed her legs and slid closer. She gazed into the cabinet and watched it like a movie screen. And memories played like a movie. The first time he'd baked her a birthday cake, the first loaf of banana bread he'd presented to her when she was sick with a cold and he'd decided she needed comfort food. Banana bread was his comfort food. The best quiche she had ever eaten. The rhubarb and strawberry pie she was sure she would not like, but did. The last loaf of sourdough bread he'd baked. The night before the accident.

Sourdough bread. The sourdough starter. She stood and swirled to face the refrigerator. She flung open the door and reached for Robert's sourdough starter. The starter his grandmother had given him and that her mother had given her. He had told Sophia that a starter was a living thing and had taught her how to feed it. A living thing passed from one baker to another, one giver of life sustaining bread to another. Sourdough starters were the essence of love, he had told her. The essence of life.

Her hands shook as she twisted the lid from the mason jar. Her hands shook as she lifted it to her nose.

This was it. It smelled yeasty and earthy. She had found it. Robert's essence. In a jar. Along with the essence of love and life. A living thing that Robert's grandmother had nurtured before she gave it to him to nurture. Some part of him that she could, and would, nurture and keep alive. And pass on. So that someone else could pass it on. And someone else. And on and on.

Christine Ahern has been writing for as long as she can remember. Poems, children's stories, short stories, novellas, and novels. She has had several short stories published in literary magazines and anthologized in several books. Her most recent publication is a novella entitled *Trudy Is the Nightbird.* Christine has worked as a custom framer, a licensed nurse, and an art store manager. She now manages one of the last remaining independent bookstores in the county. And what better way for a writer to spend her days, among books.

A HORSE RAN AMOK

Poetry by Shari Neva Hollander

A horse ran amok
Or so it seemed to those watching
But in his singular mind, it was a dash
Through spring pastures as a colt
A sprint to the finish line as a yearling
His last furlong as an old stud
Before consigning himself
To the hay in the barn and a warm blanket

Shari Neva Hollander was born a poet and that sensibility colors every aspect of her life. Even as an editor, she perceives manuscripts as symphonies that she punctuates for tempo and adds crescendos of poetic phrasing to. Although she lives in Ventura County, frequent visits to her beloved Central Coast make her feel like a dual citizen. She's the mother of a visionary son who is also a writer.

AH, BUT I WAS SO MUCH OLDER THEN; I'M YOUNGER THAN THAT NOW

Fiction by Zaslow Crane

"Ah, But I Was So Much Older Then; I'm Younger Than That Now" is an Editor's Choice selection for this issue.

It dawned on me that perhaps I'd sat too long on the park bench watching the ocean. The gulls were restive. Ground squirrels were emboldened by my quietude. They came up to my boots and looked up at me inquisitively.

Do you have any food you'd like to share? Huh? Do ya?

Some time ago, another guy had seated himself at the other end of the bench. We nodded hello, and I went back to watching the sea; he started doing whatever it was that he did. I wasn't paying attention.

Anyway, eventually, it was time to go, and my knees and hips, and maybe my ankles, were protesting that we had to move.

I may have grunted in discomfort as I got up.

I was about to nod and wave to the other guy when he said, "Hard to get old isn't it? I mean, all the things that we used to enjoy are slowly drifting out of reach. And we can watch them float away like when you're in a pool and the wind takes the floating cooler thing that holds your beer and pushes it all the way across the pool."

"Yeah, you're not wrong about that. My joints ache a bit more every day."

"And you seldom sleep all the way through the night."

"Seldom? Try, never!" We both laughed at the commonality—the unity that runs through us all, particularly two older gentlemen who were sixty-plus. Then, the guy said, "I can help you with that, you know."

"Oh yeah? What's that?"

"Getting older. You could actually be young again, if you wanted it badly enough."

I'd finally stood, and I rubbed my face anxiously.

Damn. A nutjob. Just what I need.

"Younger. Yeah. Right. Look. I gotta go."

He put a hand up. "Oh I know what you're thinking. You think I'm some crazy old fart who is off his meds."

"Something like that."

"Well, you never know. I could be. But I *could* be telling the truth." He seemed to warm to his sales pitch as if he'd done it many times in the past. He leaned in closer.

I looked at him a bit more carefully now. *I may need to identify him to the cops or something.*

He was about my age, but he was different somehow. It was as if he was some sort of person-shaped lantern, and someone had lit the wick and exposed more of the kerosene punk inside. He seemed to glow ever so slightly in the California afternoon sun. His dark brown hair was liberally streaked with gray, longish and tied behind his head with a simple scrunchy, and his clothes were nice, clean, high quality without being ostentatious. His shoes looked worn but expensive and had a nice polish on them.

No crusty deck sneakers. Interesting. He's shaved today, and it looks like he has had a shower too.

"Yeah. Okay. Thanks. Have a nice day."

"Wait."

I stopped.

"I noticed that you have age spots on your hands."

Yeah I do and they bug the crap out of me. "So?"

"So, maybe, sit back down? I may be able to help you with that at least. It won't cost you anything, and it won't take more that a minute or two."

"Why?"

"Because I want to show you that I am what I say I am. I'm not some nut job off his meds. What I am proposing is a small, simple demonstration."

"No. I don't want to—"

"They bother you a lot, don't they? Is it vanity? Or fear of skin cancer? That's not usually a very serious type of cancer though, so I'm guessing vanity."

I made a sour face.

"Is there some cream that you're gonna sell me?"

"Nope."

"Some pills that I'll have to take?"

"There is nothing but me. Sit. It'll only take a minute or two. I want to give you something to think about."

I sighed. He hadn't shown any symptoms of a guy on drugs, but these days you never know. He was, however, perfectly calm, and seemed acutely interested in persuading me.

Ok. I'll bite.

I sat. I stifled an oof of relief. *I'll admit that it felt good to sit back down.*

"Can I see your hand?"

I hesitated a bit, and he said reassuringly: "Don't *rutsch*, it won't hurt."

I put my hand in both of his. I looked down at my hand, being held by his hands, and felt a gentle but insistent warmth. I thought nothing of it until he withdrew his hands.

My hand looked 20 years younger!

I held my hand up to the optimal distance for my bifocals to focus on the hand carefully.

"It's clean. No spots, no wrinkles. How…?" I looked through the general-purpose part of the bifocals to look at him now. "Okay. This *is* quite a trick. What's the catch?"

He smiled. "I wouldn't call it a catch. The skin on your right hand— *your entire hand*—is effectively 20 years younger than the rest of your body. That's not nothing, right?"

"No. It is definitely something. It's just not possible."

"Do you disbelieve your eyes?"

"No, but…. What just happened… That can't have happened." I flexed my hands, testing them out. *Pain free!* "But…No one can make that happen."

He smiled as though he'd just handily won a hole at the local golf course. "I can." He shifted a bit before continuing. "Would you like to be thirty again? I can manage that. Younger even than that, if you're willing. I've taken people back to their teens, if that's what they wanted."

Okay. Time to go. He might be nuts; he might not be, but I don't understand what's happening right now. I've gotta absorb what just happened.

I leaned forward, hoping momentum would allow me to stand without pushing off the concrete armrest, betraying the stiffness that were the very first steps in a progression to a rather more permanent stiffness.

"Wait. You still disbelieve? Don't you even want to know how it works?"

I turned to look at him with scorn and a bit of pity.

"That was a cute trick. I don't see the upside for you. That makes me suspicious. I don't know how you did it. I'm impressed. Still, I'll see you around."

"Alright. I'll be here."

"Are you sleeping here?"

"Oh no. I just mean that I know you'll be back and, I'll wait."

I left thinking about the story I'd tell the guys in Mozzie's on Main St. tomorrow afternoon over a couple of cheap beers. – "You would not believe who I met on the bench outside "The Moonstone" yesterday!"

But I didn't.

Two days later, about the same time, and just as he said, he was waiting on *our* bench.

"Okay. You're right. My hand feels great. How'd you do it? *Why'd* you do it?"

"Hi. Nice to see you as well. It took two days for you to be intrigued enough to return? Man, you're quite a cynic, aren't you? Okay."

I lived in LA for waaay too long. I sized him up again.

"That's an interesting accent you have."

"Pennsylvania Dutch. Long ago and well in my past yet it persists." He rubbed his hands together. "As for the why, that is the easy part. It's like you won a lottery."

"I didn't enter a lottery."

"I said it's *like that*." He shook his head. "Sit down. If you're still doubting, I'll do the same thing to your left hand, if you'd like. The lottery, that's my doing and mine alone. I see people who might benefit and grow to be something more if they were given another chance. That's pretty much it."

"What's in it for you?"

"Satisfaction? I don't know, if I help you, that feels good. Isn't that enough?"

"Sadly, it isn't. I lived in LA for thirty years. I guess that I am a cynic."

"See? I knew it! Here, give me your hand and I'll explain a bit more. You're a very tough audience, you know."

LA will do that to you.

I sat and reached crossways across my body. He took my hand, and again my hand was suffused with that gentle but persistent warmth. Now I knew what to expect, so I'll admit to being excited.

"Okay." He looked into my eyes. "Here's how it works: I am a conduit by which you can shed a great many years if you choose to. After that, everything will be in apple-pie order."

I nodded. "But there's a catch."

He rolled his eyes a bit. "Yes. Yes, there is."

I yanked my hand back.

He put his hands up in a "slow down" sort of gesture.

"You're getting ahead of me, but *yes* there is … payment for this service. But I don't think calling it a catch is a fair characterization."

Here it comes. "Okay, what is it?" I crossed my arms without acknowledging that my left hand felt great. I'd pulled my hand away, and it felt hot but not unpleasant. And the spots on that hand were gone as well. In a few hours, if things progressed the way they had two days ago with my other hand, I knew that I could look forward to the arthritis easing up quite a lot.

"You pay for your youth, with your … experience. Your memories."

"What?"

"You get younger … let's for the sake of argument, let's call it twenty years. Okay?"

"Yeah."

"Well you pay for that extra time with your experiences. If you've grown smarter over the years, you'll lose twenty years worth of that smart—that experience, that knowledge."

"Whoa. I was envisioning being younger but knowing what I know now."

"Yeah that *would* be great." He chuckled ruefully. "That would be lovely, but sadly that's *not* how the process works."

"Hold up!" I was upset now. "You just did my hand; you did the other one day before yesterday. What did I pay for that treatment? Did you already take some of my knowledge? What do you want with it anyway?"

He put both hands out as if to say, "hold on, slow down, it's all good."

"Today and Monday, think of them as freebies; a way to get you to believe. And you aren't an easy one to convince."

"Could I give up childhood memories? Essentially give up those? They're worthless to me anyway." *I won't miss my childhood memories. Not a bit of them!*

"Nope. Sorry. The knowledge is peeled away in reverse order, chronologically. It's the only way I can get at them. It's like an archeological dig in some ways. The ones closest to the surface are the first ones I can get at."

Damn. "Okay, presupposing that I believe you can actually do this."

He seemed to suppress a bit of exasperation. "Don't your hands feel better? Look better? What more proof do you need? I'm offering a second chance. Youth. Vitality. I don't have infinite patience here. If you're going to be so *doplich* about all this, I'll just find someone else."

"No please. Wait. Explain. Tell me more." *Maybe somehow, this is real?*

"It's pretty straightforward: I am the conduit for you to get younger; you get younger, you lose some memories, I get my finder's fee. That's it."

"Finder's fee?"

He looked a bit sheepish. "Yeah, I get a very small portion of energy that is expended in the trade, and I get another year added onto my life."

"So, there *is* something in it for you."

"It's nominal, given the extreme benefit that you'll reap, but yeah. I get a little something for my time and efforts."

"You get a year? Every time you make someone younger? How long have you been doing this?"

He smiled. "I do. Guess how old I am."

"I don't know. Sixty-two? Sixty-three?"

He shook his head and made eye contact with me. "I'm just a *scosh* over two hundred and fifty. I'm a bit embarrassed, but I'm not at all certain of what my birthdate is. Though I remember colonial times in Pennsylvania. One of the thirteen colonies. I remember bad health, shortages, high infant mortality. I remember it all."

He'd wandered off into his memories. He then caught himself and returned to me.

"I only do one or maybe two each year. It's like treading water, trying to stay in the same place, afloat and alive. My body is thinking about failing, but just before I start to have something bad befall me, I get another infusion—from someone like you—and I buy another year."

"So, I really can be younger?"

"Yeah, but you'll give up learned experiences which is a part of you being smart, experienced, and savvy. Don't forget that part. If you agree to this, I want you to be happy and satisfied."

I wasn't convinced. Not by a long shot!

He noted my expression with wry amusement and soldiered on nonetheless.

"You'll likely have to move to another town, because when I take twenty, thirty, *forty* years away from you, someone will notice."

"Forty years?"

"Indeed, my good sir," he said archly. "If that is your wish. More if you'd like. In order to turn back the clock, to realign the hands of time, there is a price to be paid. As the Broker, I can provide the service, but the service must be paid, in full."

"Just a moment, here. Wait. I don't even know your name. Who are you?"

"You can call me Rolf."

"Okay Ralph."

"Rolf."

"Okay, *Rolf.* You're offering to make me younger? How would you do that? And for that matter, are you supposing to actually make me younger? Not just feeling better, younger. Really and truly a different, younger being?"

His eyes lit up. "Oh yes. Definitely younger. A new you. Younger, virile, more of what you were when you were much younger. Imagine being twenty-five again."

"But I'd be dumber."

"Not how I might have put it, but, yes. That's essentially it. You'll look as you did, say forty years ago, if, that is, you ask me to take almost half a century off your body for you. You'll know what you knew then."

I am not convinced, but this is an interesting thought experiment. That is, am I willing to trade one thing of value for another utterly different thing of worth? How would I gauge if this is a good trade? Being smarter as I've grown older is valuable, and there are more opportunities for younger people now, also more opportunities to get in trouble now.

When I was twenty I was a walking erection. All I thought about was sex; when I was forty all I did was work, as much as possible. All those experiences taught me valuable stuff. I'm not certain I want to give up some of the things that make me, me. And according to Rolf, I'd lose the most recent things the first—the more subtle and nuanced lessons that I've gained more recently.

I looked up at him after looking in wonder at my left hand again.

"I could be whatever age I choose?"

His eyes lit up even brighter.

"Oh, yes. Definitely younger, as young as you'd like! You'll have your life to begin anew. You're alone now, are you not? So no worries about that."

I looked directly at him this time. No more pussyfooting, I see. "How would you know that?"

He shrugged.

He began ticking off items on his fingers with his other hand's index finger. "You come and sit on this bench here around dinnertime almost every night. No missus in her right mind would stand for that, day in and day out. Yet you are not here for a liaison, nor a game of chess. You don't even feed the squirrels or gulls. And you have that look about you. You're lonely. You've lost your mate. With more time, the time I'm offering, you might find another? So, I think you are a widower. You are nearing the end of your life, and now you sit there, drinking your gin from your discrete flask, watching the waves and wondering where all the time has gone."

I felt as though he'd hit me in the face with a three-day-old carp.

He couldn't have been more on the money if he'd read my bio. *Of course, that's a confidence game trick. They usually go after widows, but why not a widower? Why not a lonely old man, seeing the light at the end of the tunnel, and knowing that the light is moving quickly towards him?*

"Alright." He continued, allowing another wrinkle into the fabric of our conversation. "There is one more thing. One more thing that I'd get, and I want to be clear about it. Included in my fee would be your memories. Someone has to keep 'em. And you can't. Not if you go backwards. You can't keep them, and I like them. Sometimes I find people's memories interesting. You would not believe the things I know from others' memories." His eyes went elsewhere for a bit, then he came back to me. "So that's my fee for services rendered."

"What makes you feel that I'd be willing to give them up?" I thought of Flora and all the good times we'd had together. Our son, who had died of yellow fever in Panama. Even bad memories were the very stuff of which I was made. *The stuff of which all of us are made.*

"I dunno. Many have. A great many over the years. It depends on how much your hips and knees hurt and how much you'd like a second chance. If you're not interested, I'll leave you be. I'm not here to *twist anyone's arm.* I'm just offering a service."

"Wait."

I can't exactly say why I stopped him from getting off the breezy bench and leaving, but I did. Gulls complained as they always do just above us. We had no food. *Why not?* they cried.

"And again, I'm not saying that I'm interested, nor that I believe you can do as you say."

At this point, a few younger men passing by had devolved into a sort of inebriated hooliganism. And a small unruly crowd surged passed us, unthinking and enveloped in drink or pot. They thankfully swept past without involving me in any of their shenanigans.

They are making memories right now.

"Why must I lose my memories?"

He pointed to the boardwalk and to the young men who by now were fifty feet away, walking and talking animatedly.

"Why must we walk on the sidewalk, or the raised planking they have here, instead of the ceiling? Why do we breathe air and not water? It is just the way things are."

He put his hands out, almost shrugging, and for the first time, I saw him, truly saw him. He seemed as perplexed at this aspect of life (such as it was) as was I.

I paused.

For some reason, I was beginning to take this weird guy seriously. I think that it was because, at least for now, he wanted nothing from me. *Except my memories. And another year's life. Hah!* I chuckled to myself.

I'll take him up on this offer and see what happens. And if nothing happens, it might be worth the trouble to turn this old SOB into the cops.

I gripped my walking stick a bit more tightly than was necessary as this thought sent a slight thrill of adventure through me.

"I need to go feed my dog. She gets cranky if she isn't fed by five."

"And they always know when it's five, don't they?"

"Oh yeah! Let's wait. I'm gonna go home and think hard about this (and flex my hands!). Let's meet tomorrow at Mozzie's around two, after the lunch drunks' rush. We'll talk then. Okay?"

He'd stood as I was talking. "Okay. See you there."

I looked up. "Two at Mozzie's. I'll be there. Not promising anything, but I'll be there."

At home, I looked around. Not much had changed since Flora's passing almost four years ago. The drapes, which she had picked out and been so happy with, now seemed drab and colorless; the furniture was somehow emptier now that only one of us sat on the couch.

Molly the dachshund met me at the door expecting to be fed, so I obliged her.

My entire hand, not simply the skin on that hand, truly felt better. All the aches and pains that just snipe at you when you least expect it were gone. My hands felt great!

"What about you Molly? Would you still recognize me if I was changed by this guy?" Molly looked at me quizzically and then returned to her bowl—I'd put in some of yesterday's meat loaf, and I knew she loved that, so I didn't expect her to pay any more attention to me so long as that was there. "How would you feel, girl? I mean if I got younger and you stayed … well … older? Would you feel cheated?"

Oh my god, would I forget Flora? If I went back far enough, I would! I don't know if I could bear that! And Timothy! We loved him so much. We supported each other to get over his passing. I'd forget him too if I really did this. On the other hand, what an opportunity! There is precious little for me here and now.

On the wall was a grouping of the three of us hiking in the Andes. *Those pictures will be like they're of someone else if I do this.* Sadly, I looked around the empty kitchen. The only sounds were a clock ticking and Molly finishing up her dinner. "So. What do you think, Molly? Should I do it? It's quite a trade!"

Molly was no help with my quandary.

It was two o'clock. I walked into Mozzie's. He smiled. His expression said, "Another happy customer."

We had a beer each and sat way at the end of the long lacquered bar, away from everyone else and somewhat enveloped in the semi-secrecy of the wash of jukebox speakers.

I leaned as if imparting some great secret, some conspiracy. *The same great secret or conspiracy everyone has to deal with, eventually.* "You know, part of me wants this, wants this badly. But another part of me thinks that I'll be giving up everything that makes me, *me*. My memories, my experiences … after all, that's all we really are, aren't we? A product of our experience and remembrances? If I agree, I'll lose an important part of me. I'll get incrementally more stupid. I'm smart now. I don't think I want to get stupid, go backwards. I worked hard for what I know."

Rolf nodded and his eyes said that he understood. "I will value what I take from you. The knowledge will not be lost."

"It'll be lost from me!"

"At least it won't be wasted."

"Uh, yeah, nature herself will take that from me soon enough. Then, it *will* be wasted! Maybe if I see a failing getting more pronounced I might take you up on this, but I just can't throw away perfectly good memories when I'm still in fairly good shape."

He sighed and drained his beer.

"Well, I'm sorry that you could see no value in this. Many others have."

"Wait. I didn't say no. I just said that I didn't want to lose a big part of me."

"But that is the only way."

"Oh, I understand what you're saying, but there still may be another way forward."

I signaled for two more drafts. We were quiet as the beers were delivered. He now seemed quite intrigued. He waited for me to continue as he took a slow, small sip of the amber liquid.

"I think I'd would like you to turn back time for me."

He smiled.

"But for one day, just one day. I haven't learned anything momentous today. I can spare that knowledge. Make me one day younger."

"But that will not benefit you."

"It will."

"How?"

"It   will benefit *you*."

"What?"

"If you induct me into this very rarified society, you'll get another year doing what you do, right?"

"Yes."

"Well, the way I see it, I may not be a great candidate because I'm too in love with the knowledge I've gained. You're doing a good thing, giving a second chance to someone who might rewind and do something better in his new life. But that's not for me—not now, anyway. If I do this, as I understand this, this keeps you alive and maybe helping someone truly in need. I think what you do is admirable."

"Really?"

"Yeah. Why not? Think about it. What do you get? Another year and some weird memories that have no context? By the way, I want my memories. I don't want anyone else to have them. No offense."

"None taken." He waited. "So?"

"So, take me back to yesterday. Anytime you take away someone's experiences and memories and years, you get a year? Right?"

"Yes, but—"

"That'll be sufficient for you to get what you need, and I'll get another day, which I promise you, I will enjoy."

I looked around to emphasize my thought. Just outside the dim bar was sun, sand, sea, seagulls ... pretty good stuff...

He looked mystified and a bit grateful.

I continued. "Maybe we'll run into each other again, and maybe I'll be feeling something different then."

He nodded and shared a gentle, placid smile. "Maybe. And thank you." He seemed to be starting to tear up, so I got up, and asked, "How does this work?"

"Follow me."

The process knocked me out and I woke up at home. Molly lay next to me as if worried.

The guys down at Mozzie's would never believe me when I told them this tale, but they'd argue for the rest of the day over how far back *they'd* go.

I went to *my* bench and sat and watched the waves. It's astounding how calming that is, at least for me. In a little while, Rolf came and sat at the far end of the bench.

"You look well," I offered.

"So do you."

"So are you down here to watch the tide again?" I asked.

"No. I'm leaving here soon, and I just wanted to say thanks."

"Thanks? For what?"

He sighed. "It's too hard to explain, so just Thanks."

I chuckled a bit.

"You're welcome, I guess, for whatever."

"Maybe I'll see you again sometime."

"Yeah. Maybe."

"Like maybe next year." At this, he waved, stood up, and walked away.

Next year? That's oddly specific. I watched him walk away. *The whack jobs are more common, but better dressed these days.*

Then, absently, I flexed my hands. They felt *great.*

Zaslow Crane has published 11 books of fiction. He was the primary writer (as well as producer and host) for the parsec-award nominated podcast *Smoke and Mirrors: Reimagining The Twilight Zone.* He has contributed to dozens of industry magazines (cooking, in-flight, photography, training). He has been published in *Galaxy's Edge*, *Sci-Fi Lampoon*, *Unidentified Funny Objects* and several other sci-fi magazines, books, and online 'zines. He's received multiple honorable mentions from L. Ron Hubbard's Writers of the Future. He is currently working on a humor book, posting one cartoon at a time on Facebook to be compiled into one very silly volume in the near future.

THE POTTER

Poetry by Joe Amaral

Before enlightenment, chop wood, carry water.
After enlightenment, chop wood, carry water. —Zen proverb

In the brooderhouse,
the farmer stares
at a digital clock
whose red slashes

smile
3:AM

He finishes
spinning clay,
squeezing wet bricks
out white barrels.

Wheel-throwing mugs,
vases, and candelabras.
Come daylight he tends
chickens, splits cords

of firewood and rides
a tractor over hose-damp soil
slow—plowing components
of his own grave. The kiln

fires a rainbow glaze.
Hardening wares
into quaint arrays
like war-torn flags

of misplaced countries
with mythical species. He noshes
fava beans by the potbelly
stove, feeding bits of kindling

and yellow newspaper
into the cast-iron surrounded
by cats and aged carpet,
Portuguese bull-riding posters

above cerulean sofas who sigh
blue dust in wistful comfort.

A black and white television
mewls at him, silver antennae
never straight enough
to combat the static. The farmer

closes his eyes, letting these creases
of a well-lived life
sculpture him in fine
undercoats of earth, hearth,

and feline purrs, the brooderhouse rooster alert
for the egg crack of dawn:
a sepulchral sunrise—

a malleable shape.

EULOGY FOR PA POPS

Poetry by Joe Amaral

*There is a time for everything, and a season for every activity under the heavens: a
time to be born and a time to die, a time to plant and a time to uproot. —*
Ecclesiastes 3:1-2

He passed peacefully on an early spring afternoon,
his fruit trees in full bloom, winter crops seeding
near rows of fava beans ready for harvest.

Ninety-five years old bobbing for apples in metal troughs.

Some live a long life good enough,
others a good life long enough.
Mel lived good and long.

Dad, Papa, *Vovo*, Pa Pops: Melvin Amaral was born in 1917 Oakland.
He huddled in Castro Valley with family members
during the Depression, primarily raising chickens
and eventually building a poultry farm in Hayward
on an apricot tree orchard.

It was on Meekland Estate property
with an eighty-foot well from the Mount Diablo watershed
kept running with lots of care, oil, and a gravity-fed tank house.
He never tasted city water nor tested that well for chemicals,
trusting the earth underneath to sustain him.
Mel was an accomplished welder and inventor, turning
scraps of old machinery into necessary equipment.

He gathered seeds, tilled the land tenderly, and knew how to reap
and provide for his family, share with his community, and cook,
can, dry, juice, and compost his fruits and vegetables
to utilize every shred of woolen life he spun loose.

Mel married Mary Mendonca and they belonged to
the Pacific Growers Credit Union, and later the All Saints
Senior Center while watching their family grow and grow

like giant pumpkins and corn mazes, successfully combating
the weeds, wars, and economic obstacles in their way.

Mel and Mary belonged to Portuguese Lodges and camping
groups, loved to fish and smoke salmon in Fort Bragg,
clam at Pismo Beach, and travel the world, including the place
their parents migrated from: the Azores Islands.

They worked hard all day, but on weekends, they danced.

THE ANTIQUITY OF YOUTH

Poetry by Joe Amaral

1.

I scry through ancient farm walls
of warped scrap wood, rustic as concentric
heart rings; a crenulated tin man.

Unripe blackberries dangle
off oxidized trellises. Emaciated
figs, brazenly sour oranges.

Along rows of blighted tomato vines
I mire in stagnant trenches
once irrigated by the leaking tank house.

Sit astride tractors that no longer run,
black grease viscous, congealing
in prolonged stasis like hay ricks.

I peel paint chips and sponge rot,
sleep in sawdust, inhale the discoloration
of dull bandsaws and blades.

2.

As a boy I ran with my sheepdog
up and down long chicken pens
under the silent appraisal of bunnies,
listening to echoes of rooster crow,
honk of irate geese and bleat of new lambs
still getting their gangly legs under them.

Multitudes of feral cats mousing
and birding and sunning and sleeping.

Atop aluminum coop roofs I jumped into
musty haystacks, running back and forth among

tools and machines and soil! So much soil
full of weeds or plowed to dark chunks seeded
with so many vegetables I could hate
the taste of half but still have dozens to enjoy.

3.

Then the well ran dry.

I drank it up growing big and hearty,
hit my stride and instead of sagging
and wilting and giving back to beckoning
dirt; recycle, mulch, replant,
I kept aging and didn't rejoin
the cyclical particles comprising
the farm's starving existence

until it was too late.

4.

The farm bore my play, my antics.
Put up with my solo missions
of destruction; bemused at the mud
and blood and scars and small hurts
I accumulated in headstrong heedlessness.

It waited for me when I moved away.

It waited for personhood.

I never returned.

Where does land forgotten fall?
Oceanic myth? Disingenuous dust …
winds afraid to wail what is happening.
Suffocated in disrepair, it returns
to a natural state unnatural to us.

5.

We idolize old barns as relics of times past:
I see them as failures of man—
of myself.

Only in poetic dreams does my childhood
recede from adult imprisonment.
It was beautiful.   It is a funeral.

I scry through ancient farm walls
of warped scrap wood, rustic as concentric
heart rings; a crenulated tin man.

Joe Amaral's first poetry collection *The Street Medic* won the 2018
Palooka Press Chapbook Contest. His writing has appeared in *Anti-
Heroin Chic*, *Last Leaves Magazine*, *Please See Me*, *Rise Up Review*, *River Heron
Review*, *The Night Heron Barks*, and *University Professors Press*. Joe works
forty-eight-hour shifts as a paramedic on California's Central Coast. He
can be found on Instagram @joeticmedic.

THE GOLDEN QUILL WRITING CONTEST

The 2024 Golden Quill Writing Contest awarded cash prizes and publication in *The NightWriter Review* to the first and second place winners in the categories of fiction, nonfiction, and poetry.

The annual writing contest is hosted by SLO NightWriters, a California Central Coast writing organization with a mission to advance quality writing, promote publication, and expand author recognition in a forum that nurtures a spirit of community for all its members.

Thank you to our judges: *New York Times* bestselling author of the *Gangsterland* series, Tod Goldberg (fiction), award-winning author of *The Curious Reader's Field Guide to Nonfiction*, Anne Janzer (nonfiction), and former San Luis Obispo County poet laureate and author of the poetry collection *Wind and Hills*, Marguerite Costigan(poetry).

Thank you to the writers who entered for trusting us with your work. Our 2025 Golden Quill Writing Contest opens April 1, 2025. For details, visit **SLO**Night**Writer**.org or The**Night**Writer**Review**.com.

Congratulations to this years winners, as chosen from the finalists by outside judges Tod Goldberg, Anne Janzer, and Marguerite Costigan.

FICTION

First Place: Sounds like Joni Mitchell by S.S. Presby
Second Place: The Lila Segovia Smile by Anne R. Allen

Fiction Finalists:

Confession by JD McKay
Cozy Life by the Rock by M. Golda Turner
Devil Cut by Robert Morgan Fisher
Growing up in White and Black by Jack Cameron
Man to Man by Shena Crane
Remnants of Love by Sharyl Heber
Simulation by Arthur M. Doweyko
The Essence by Christine Ahern

NONFICTION

First Place: My Favorite Animal is a Harbor Seal by Michele L. Roest
Second Place: My Wrinkled Brain by Rusty Evans
Honorable Mention: The Stoic Parent by T.K. Schuberth

<u>Nonfiction Finalists</u>:

A Pool Runs Through It by Susan Chase
Flirty Hemlines by Nikol Rochez
Mother-Daughter Luncheon by Debra Davis Hinkle
Ninety Miles From Normal by Christina Dillow
Origin Story by Dona M. Hare Price
Seasons of an American Striver by Patricia Garrison
What's Love Got To Do With It? by Thomas Brauner
What They Brought by Maryann Grau

POETRY

First place: Anatomy of a Train by L.I. Henley
Second place: Game Time by B. Misty Wycoff

<u>Poetry Finalists</u>:

Cynthia Remembered by Judith Amber
December 1972 by Lewis H. Leicher
Memories by Tina Niebuhr
Ode to My First Car by Deborah Tobola
Racism by Sari H. Dworkin
Spring Trip to the Lake by Nancy Yang
The Potter by Joe Amaral
The Wish by Margaret Christine Lang